RUNNING WITH OUR EYES CLOSED

RUNNING WITH OUR EYES CLOSED

a novel

Mel Greenberg

Tucson, Arizona

Running With Our Eyes Closed

This book is a work of fiction. Any references to historical events, people, or real locales are used fictitiously.

Published by 4 Pillars Publishing,
a division of MEL Media, LLC,
Tucson, Arizona

For permissions and information, visit melmediallc.com

Running With Our Eyes Closed

Hardcover ISBN 978-1-7321015-2-4
Paperback ISBN 978-1-7321015-1-7
E-book ISBN 978-1-7321015-0-0

Library of Congress Control Number: 2018903311

Editing by Kate McCormick
Cover art and design by Amelia Noyes, amelianoyesdesign.com
Author Photo by Dominic Arizona Bonucceli
Interior book design by DTPerfect.com

For **Jacqueline Rose Arledge**

You taught me to believe in my dreams and myself
and to never, ever give up.

VENICE
ITALY
FLORENCE
ROME

"What is the fatal charm of **Italy**?
What do we find there that can be found
nowhere else? I believe it is a certain
permission to be **human** . . ."

ERICA JONG

CONTENTS

Introduction

I first met Mel Greenberg by chance at our family's leather shop in Florence in 2012. We shared an immediate connection, our love of family and life. Over the years, that friendship has evolved, as we have evolved as women and mothers.

I've lived in Florence for 18 years, but Mel captured and described things that took me years to understand while living here and integrating into the society and culture. Her perspective is not limited to the Florentine one . . . she writes with a general sensitivity that represents women all over the world. The Florentine women DO talk at Rivoire, and it's typical Florentine talk, *"Live in the moment."* There are no straight answers for any questions, just more and more questions for reflection.

Mel takes readers on an authentic journey into the rebirth of a woman, Samantha, within the coulisse of the Renaissance city par excellence, Florence. Her character's journey is both the dream of a young girl and the nightmare of a more realized mature woman. If we're mothers, we make sure our children fly safely from the nest before we go back to our professions and start discovering ourselves. As women, we often dare to tread lightly for the fear of tasting success and discovering the real 'us'!

Mel's book taught me that by raising children, I'm not missing anything and life is not passing me by. I am grateful for what the Italian lifestyle has also taught me — how Florentians slow down to taste and savor each moment. I can see each one of us somewhere in Samantha's thoughts and in her behavior! Love is never black and white. Samantha and Michael move back and forth so much between anger and love and hope and resolve that the reader never knows — maybe it's over OR maybe they can work it out.

Her book is a remedy for my soul — La Belle Vita!

Dr. Sana Barada
Florence, Italy

"I'll be there, **always.**

Because nothing else matters

when you can run back to **love.**"

Florence, Italy

MONDAY, MARCH 13, 2017

Breathe . . . just fucking breathe . . . Letting her eyes roll shut, Samantha inhaled, a long, slow, deep breath, then another and another, allowing each to settle in her stomach before releasing the air with a rush. She struggled to calm her nerves as the the air flowed through her, allowing herself to fall back against the door of the rickety old bathroom stall, while she watched scenes from the last 72 hours pass across the inside of her eyelids. Blurred images of a life that seemed to be crumbling at her feet. Three days, beginning with three words that would change her forever. *What am I doing here, what are we doing here?* She opened her eyes with a final, exaggerated breath, savoring the aroma of the rain as it landed on the concrete. The mineral-infused concoction floated back up, providing a healing elixir of calm. How, she wondered, did she end up here, feeling like such an imposter. Her exterior of strength and conviction shielding her fragile interior, a child herself, so unsure of everything. How could it be that you move through life so sure of who you are and what your purpose is — then seemingly and with no warning end up in a free-fall down the rabbit hole with absolutely no confidence or belief in yourself? All good questions she thought as she continued to ponder her fate, family and future.

Samantha rested on the seat, head in hands, the wind shaking the shutters behind her as erratically as her thoughts poured through her, seeking solace in the confines of the water closet. A tiny structure, with faded yellow paint chipped away at the corners, and a narrow window above the ledge just behind her, where she'd mindlessly tossed her purse before sitting down. It was the kind she remembered from grade school, frosted, double paned glass over wire mesh, framed with beveled wood and a corroded brass lock barely holding the two pieces together. A slight bang of the door interrupted her vigil. Samantha turned and looked up, then back at the stall door in front of her and took a deep breath; at first to tangle with the onset of anxiety she was feeling, but then to savor the scent she now recognized, the musk cologne dancing in the air. She imagined the beads of sweat dripping off his forehead and it was comforting actually. Though a different kind of anxiety quickly took over as she considered the hand turning the knob on the door.

Samantha desperately wanted to escape the questions and problems plaguing her life at this moment. Close the door, lock it up and leave it in the past. At least on the surface that's how it felt to her. But, as life does, things turn and twist, changing in an instant life as she'd known it. And here she was now, in the middle of Florence, having to face those consequences head on. She simply had no plan of action for what lay ahead. Yet here she was, separated by inches of worn metal from the man who'd stolen her heart in ways she'd never imagined, in a country that had done the same, decades ago. Hardly where she expected to be and certainly not how she'd ever dreamt it might happen.

Samantha nervously tried to stand and gain her composure. The door she thought was securely locked rode the turbulent afternoon breeze to settle just slightly ajar. Admittedly somewhat surprised, she was expecting a more dramatic gesture — the door would fly open railing against the brick wall to its right and there he'd be. But no, a gentle prod seemed to unlatch the gloriously archaic hardware and the door swung open, unceremoniously. Just a slight screech of opposition from the screws rubbing against the latch they were barely holding in place. And in the minutes that followed Samantha threw caution to the wind, leaving behind every sense of virtue and dignity she'd ever aspired to maintain. She braced herself, looked up and drank in the shimmer of his deep hazel eyes, cherishing the moment, lost in the magic of how simple love could feel.

"Hi," Samantha whispered, enveloped in vulnerability looking up at Michael. *Oh Jesus, are you kidding?!* she thought, assailing herself with disgust and frustration as she moved clumsily about the seat. Samantha lived in her head. She wrote and rewrote every conversation she ever had with herself long before the words ever left her lips to take on a life of their own. Of course, more often than not, those scripts remained safely tucked away, never seeing the light of day, serving purely as a means to address her life's ever-changing plot lines. Now, face to face with an unfolding fantasy even she did not fully comprehend, she was incapable of calling up the best stream of witty dialogue she'd so easily authored.

"What are you doing, this is crazy? Someone might come in here!" Samantha made one final attempt at communicating. Michael closed the door behind him, cradled both of her shoulders in his warm, generous hands, pulled her to her feet and kissed her. His moist lips were warm and soft and they fit, so easily they fit. She barely noticed her shorts falling to the floor. Samantha took inventory of the man in front of her, strong, self-assured and so damn sexy. She felt his energy, a pulse that she couldn't escape. There was a sense of urgency to the encounter, one Michael was fully aware he was fueling. He wanted and needed her, right then and there. "Exactly what you want me to do — what I want to do." Michael answered with bravado, believing without question that she felt exactly the same way. "Living on the edge, where we like it, right? Where we can let it all go, no regrets." She'd revisit those words, over and over again in the days to come, but for now, she did just that . . .

Samantha responded the only way she knew how — no words — just feeling and action. A pattern of behavior that, while usually giving her the thrill she sought, was not always one that served her best interests and well-being. Falling backwards onto the seat, she deftly unbuckled his belt. Then with what seemed like one swift movement, she unzipped his shorts, letting them slide down his tanned, muscular thighs, pulling his boxers to one side to reveal that beautiful growing piece. She savored and stroked it, gently at first. Her tongue ached to touch the flickering muscle in her hand. Licking, at first in short strokes, followed by a long, easy slide between her lips. She savored the sweet taste, slowly sucking his grandeur until Michael nearly collapsed from the ecstasy she was creating between his legs. Feeling his rise, Samantha let out a moan that provoked Michael's release. She shuddered as he slowly pulled out, leaving her mouth full, her knees withered and weak. Michael leaned back on the stall door, eyes closed.

Samantha watched him silently, once again scanning his body head to toes, wondering where his thoughts had taken him. His breathing was still heavy and his hands still held her shoulders tightly. His grip was different now, strong but somehow relieved, as though the weight of his world had been lifted. It was a reassuring and frightening moment for her. Was this man her future? Could the past really be so easily rewritten? Water, bridges, closing doors: she envisioned all the cliches that described the proverbial fork in the road where she now stood. She remained still, watching him as his eyes slowly opened, locking solidly on her gaze. It was perhaps the closest she'd ever felt to him. Kneeling down to get his shorts, Samantha looked up and caught his smile, "God I love the fuck out of you. See you outside." He zipped up, flashed his addictive grin and eased out of the stall.

There's charm in mistakes, she thought as she sat back down in the stall, not quite ready for public consumption. Undistracted by her surroundings, Samantha savored this rare moment to be present, to consider her actions past and present and hell, to relish what had just been mind-blowing sex in a bathroom stall in Florence, Italy! How many had preceded her, she wondered. Had this minute space served as a rendezvous for clandestine lovers for decades past? Re-igniting lost flames, fanning those of new love? She felt curiously entrenched in both scenarios. This was a beginning of sorts as well as an ending. She'd given in, let go and had a damn good time doing it. Fuck, and there it was, the smack back to reality — her impulsive nature — the gypsy spirit she so cherished, the attraction for so many, and the devil within. Any number of excuses worked, but Samantha knew that while her current situation did not rest solely on her shoulders, the choices made were not done so with the long-term, best interests of anyone involved being considered. That was easily the biggest challenge at hand, going forward. Was there sufficient evidence of change, could she move on, committing to Michael, to a life they could build together from here? Was she ready for the next and really, the final act of her life? Was it with him?

With questions that could not possibly be answered at this moment, she pulled herself together and stepped from the stall. Looking down, she straightened her shirt, unaware of the mirror directly in front of her. As she tugged at her shorts her eyes followed her head upward staring straight into her reflection in the dusty, cracked glass. There she was again, the teenage girl she'd lost touch with so long ago when being invisible was her only means of survival, standing next to the woman she was today. Feeling like a fraud, she applied a touch of lip gloss and stared. It was a profound assemblage of imagery. Disheveled and cracked, but surrounded by unmatched beauty. Exactly how she felt to her core. These were her life's contradictions — a beautiful childhood, unraveled over the passage of time and lost connection — a present wrought with deception, unsatisfied expectations — a future filled with so much uncertainty. But maybe that uncertainty would be the catalyst to fit all the pieces back together. Samantha fingered the layers of her wavy, shoulder-length blonde hair and left those thoughts, and the memory of the glorious, albeit somewhat careless encounter behind, strolling confidently into the now crowded restaurant and out to Michael.

"How is it that we end up here?

Are we all just a **hopelessly**,

broken tangled mess?"

Florence, Italy

FRIDAY, MARCH 10, 2017

3 Days Earlier . . .

The sky over the city had taken on a captivating tone on this sultry Friday afternoon. Much more varied than usual, given the early hour, and it was considerably warm for this time of year. The days leading into spring, everything is new, coming to light, alive with hope. Samantha pondered this as she stepped onto the patio of Rivoire, on the Piazza della Signoria, stopping to savor both the view and the moment at one of her favorite restaurants. There was a slight chill in the air but the sky, its faint blue canvas saturated with frenetic strokes of red, orange and gold, intrigued her. They were at odds with each other. No gentle brushstrokes sweeping across the horizon, as she'd witnessed in so many prior Florentine sunsets. Emotionally, this day was coming to a visual end much as it had begun, devastatingly raw and antagonistically charged. If only the setting sun could also lay to rest the conflicts that were rising full force within her.

"Ahhhh," she sighed, shaking her head slowly taking it all in. Samantha was standing steadfast in the middle of a true paradox. Feet solidly planted on the cobblestone patio of her most cherished city, feeling anything but grounded. This dance, a friction deep inside, was gnawing at her in a way she could no longer contain. At least that is what she wrestled with now as she looked across the patio at the tables occupied by couples, actively engaged, in love as she saw it and what she had not truly felt in ages. Then there were the friends, sipping cocktails, talking, laughing together, leaving her longing for the true, lifelong friendships she'd let slide in recent years. How, she wondered, had her life ended up here, seemingly overnight, though she knew perfectly well it had been a long and slow descent in to what she viewed as her own personal hell. *I'll take some of the blame,* she thought, almost saying it out loud. *But fuck if I'm owning all of it anymore. This has got to give, I've got to get these feelings out of me, I'm suffocating.* She tugged at her neckline, feeling the emotions with each breath. So much easier to say to herself, no consequences. Bold, empowered, in control — traits Samantha admired and strived for, but had tucked away long ago. Raising their three children, supporting all of Michael's ventures and dreams, it all worked — until it didn't. She was here now and facing her crossroads. It was time to come forward, to use the voice she'd quieted for so many years. A whisper emerged from her pursed lips, a look she didn't know she'd taken on while considering her plight. How strange she must look to those unwitting characters sitting on the patio watching her. The thoughts running through her head took over her physical being before she even realized it. She felt tight, fists and jaw clenched, brow furrowed, eyes welling up with tears, her angry mouth pulsating. Samantha quickly took inventory of her surroundings. *Pull your shit together girl — you're being ridiculous!* But, a faint whisper emerged from those quivering lips, "Help me . . . "

The waiter passing at just that moment responded, "A table signora?"

Shit, Samantha thought, *that's embarrassing — hot mess alert, no self control.*

"No, no grazie, I'm waiting for my husband, just heading into the bar."

The flight over on Thursday was long and she was still tired. She was used to the trip, having done it so often, over so many years, but today's *"flight hangover"* was really taking its toll. She preferred taking the train up from Rome, but Michael had insisted on sending their plane. She had to admit, now she was glad he did — it gave her more time to herself before connecting with him. Of course she knew, more than anything, she was emotionally exhausted. She was glad to have had the day to herself to recover. Michael's day was full of meetings for their new development about 30 kilometers southeast of the city center. They'd planned to meet here for a drink before catching up with Michael's business partner Carlo and his wife Stefania for dinner. Samantha made reservations at SESTO, the rooftop restaurant at the Excelsior, a favorite of hers for the view of the Arno and the gardens across the river. He was late and that was a bit unusual. Or maybe she was just more tuned in to his absence because of all that she was contemplating. Was she looking for fault, for shortcomings? Wouldn't that make it all so much easier! She conceded that a great deal of her angst was directly related to the current state of their relationship. Almost a duty, she felt, not looking forward to their evening at all. Did he feel it as deeply as she did? Surely, this was not as one-sided as he often argued, working so hard, it seemed, to convince her that this was just how life and marriage played out after so many years together. It was natural to feel somewhat distant and "off", he loved to preach. Michael often approached these conversations from an "I've experienced so much more than you" angle. An effort, Samantha felt was an attempt to minimize her complaints and concerns. An effort that he generally succeeded in accomplishing. *Well,* she thought, *I'm not buying it anymore. There is no way he's happy either and I'm fucking sick of him telling me it's me. Telling me to 'get over it — you have an amazing life, stop looking for trouble.' It's not amazing, it sucks and you're a part of it. We suck, we have for months now. You just won't deal with it.*

Samantha turned on her heels, empowered slightly by her inner dialogue, ready to make her way to the bar to wait for his arrival. She took two determined steps, before glancing back once more, no sight of him. She cursed herself, in the midst of feeling such dismay for their present status, she missed him and wanted him desperately. Still no Michael, so she decided to embrace the moment, to take it all in, alone. She gazed up once more at the sky, now decidedly saying goodnight to the day's sun. The once brightly shimmering horizon was dimly lit by the lights of the town and the sun's afterglow. Shadows cast an iridescent luster across the sky, offering the gently rising moon center stage.

A slow, deep inhale brought an instant smile to her lips. First, the freshly baked pizza being served to a table on her right, followed by a delicate breeze of Grain de Soleil perfume coming from a table just behind her. Ahhhh, the warm blend of earthy notes, she knew it well because Diamont, also from perfumery Fragonard, had become her signature scent. Michael had given it to her a year or so before. It was love at first spray: down to earth, yet unmistakably bright and striking. She liked to think of herself that way: an irresistible sparkle, lingering long after she'd left the room. Samantha was especially drawn to Fragonard's rich and passionate history. Eugene Fuchs was an entrepreneur seduced by perfume's magical essence. Named after the French artist Jean-Honore Fragonard, Fuchs opened the legendary perfumery in 1926 in Grasse, France. Three generations later, Fragonard stood above the masses in producing not just the finest fragrances, but in selling art and history along the way. For Samantha it was this type of attention to detail and the honoring of long-held tradition that captured and kept her interest in most things throughout her life.

She followed the scent, her curiosity piqued as it was unique, such a distinct bouquet. She listened intently as two women commiserated over their newly poured champagne, the arpeggio of bubbles clearly audible and worthy of the Florentine landscape. The woman wearing Soleil was elegant, simply stunning. Blonde, older she thought, closer to Michael's age of 58. The 11 years between them had never been more of an issue than during the past months.

Her evolving interests and needs significantly altered the state of their relationship. Inhaling this stranger's scent now, observing her delicate, chic demeanor, Samantha considered her own age in a negative light for the first time. Wondering if she might ever embody such grace and ease. *Perhaps,* she thought, *it's a cultural gift I will just never have.* Feeling a bit guilty eavesdropping, but unable to tear herself away, Samantha slowly tuned out everything around her but these two women, friends, sisters, companions, the nature of their relationship wasn't clear, but it appeared this Friday afternoon was for celebrating . . . something. What, her curiosity on fire, made this day so special? Her proficiency in Italian translation now hard at work, Samantha strained to hear more.

"How it all comes together," the blonde's companion said, gesturing her hands in grand fashion, reaching to the sky, welcoming it in. "When we are most in fear and feeling so very lost — ahhhh yes my friend, that is when the clouds clear and our journey shifts." She laughed vigorously, then placed her right hand on the left forearm of the blonde woman and the conversation took a quiet, more serious turn.

"I've been so lost since Emilio left," the blonde woman continued, "I question everything: my life, my love, my dreams. What did I do wrong, why did he look for another love. Was I just so out of touch with our world, our life as a couple? Did I do this to us? Was I to blame? Maybe I did fail him, our marriage. I don't know . . . Yes I do . . ." She chuckled a bit, "I didn't fail him, I stayed — I tried — I loved him and he left me. That's just what it is and I know that now. Thank God I have Gabriella, she's been such a source of strength. My beautiful daughter, she should never have had to weather this storm. We all make our choices, consequences be damned. But then there are the tomorrows . . . nothing is ever what it seems and hardly perfect. But he chose to leave, to give up on us so that's on him." She pulled her hand away grasping her left wrist to support her chin as she looked off in the distance, across the Piazza.

"Pffffttt" the friend replied, spitting dry air to the ground, "he is not worthy of mention! But now, look at you my love, you are alive again! It is time indeed to smile and live your life. I adore him, even though he is American!" She threw her head back in exaggerated laughter. "He is everything you deserve now. Be happy, unapologetic! This is your time." She brought all ten fingers to her mouth, kissed them and flung them skyward, releasing the wish. She leaned in to her friend, catching her bracelet on the table cloth, shaking it a bit, and in what was more of a whisper continued, "We are all to blame in some way, but I think blame is not the right term. More that we are all players in this very complicated game of life. Sometimes our responses don't fit, other times they fit precisely, but not for the outcome we desire. And sometimes, my love, they simply take on a life of their own and we lose sight of all that matters to us, until it is too late." She reached across the table now, wrapping both of her friend's hands in hers, a show of strength and reassurance that her friend was not on the journey alone. "This, I suspect, will be that scoundrel's realization once he sees you have chosen to live and be happy without him."

The blonde looked at her friend with deep affection and fear, it seemed. "But what am I really getting myself into. He has a wife, a family. I know he says it's over but is any of that ever really over?"

She paused, sipping her drink as her companion responded, "No, not likely. But, Carolina, you didn't look for this. It came to you, he came to you, I think at this time, to save you and maybe himself as well. You've been through so much. Stop looking for explanations and approval, just live with it and enjoy the time you are given."

"I suppose," Carolina conceded. "Though I am somewhat circumspect, I don't know that I want all the baggage that this relationship will undoubtedly bring. But, then again, we are beautifully suited, we do bring each other such joy, so . . . ." She glanced at her watch, "I'm meeting him shortly, he said he desperately needed to talk with me this afternoon. Maybe, finally . . . " Her hopeful voice trailed off.

"Exactly!" the friend interrupted, satisfied to see her friend coming to the conclusion she envisioned was her best course of action. "Just live, be — please enjoy yourself for now."

Of course that's her name, Samantha smirked to herself. *Everything about this woman exudes sheer Italian refinement, why would her name be anything less?* She lost track of their conversation momentarily while she contemplated what she'd witnessed.

What a beautiful sight, unconditional, loyal friendship. I wish Kelly were here. I'll call her later. Kelly was not only her older sister, but her best friend. She'd be unforgiving and candid in her opinion. That was her inescapable gift, to a fault at times, the truth. Cold, hard, funny, painful authenticity, Kelly would only accept that from her sister, from anyone really. She was impatient with the dance people did to save face or spare feelings. Probably why she was still single. That notion brought a smile to Samantha's lips, followed by a much louder gasp, startling all three women. Carolina and her companion looked up at her, glaring somewhat, then easing into a questioning stare. Who was this woman listening so intently to their conversation. Unaware of how far she'd leaned in to hear their words, their peculiar gaze caught her off guard. Embarrassed, she struggled to remove herself as quickly as possible from the horribly awkward situation. Backing into a waiter, Samantha seized the inconvenience of the mishap to redirect her attention, and that of the two women, turning away quickly to apologize to him. He knew her well, and gently escorted her inside to the bar. *Oh for God's sake!* she thought, *he must have seen what I was doing, the whole damn patio for that matter. How rude they must think I am, stupid American,* her inner dialogue was wrought with humiliation and anger.

Paulo, the adorable waiter who had attended to her and Michael so lovingly over the years could see how distraught she was. Though with no idea of the depth of the frustration and self-loathing that was looping in her head, he sat her down at the bar and brought her a glass of the Amarone she always ordered. How ironic, she considered as she stared into the glass in front of her encircling the rim with the tip of her finger. The wine she coveted originated in the Valpolicello area of Veneto in northeastern Italy. The very region that inspired Shakespeare to write Romeo and Juliet's tragic love story.

Samantha reached in her purse for lip gloss, running each finger over the binding of her journal. She pulled it out and started to read what she'd written earlier in the day. She'd begun the practice as a teenager, so many years ago, filling the pages with whatever inspired her during her stay. Letters home, not sent, she used to tell herself, confessions that would never be heard. The entries revealed her deepest thoughts, she kept several books in the hotel safe, collecting the most current edition upon her arrival. There were 22 now — beautifully bound leather books, tied neatly shut with gold twine. Someday, she presumed, they'd be read. They may be revered or reviled, she'd leave that to those who came after, but they exposed every fragment of who she had been and who she had become. Who she was now had changed dramatically from the young girl, poised on the edge of adulthood, who had put pen to paper more than a quarter of a century ago. She barely knew that girl anymore. *Where in the hell did she go,* she contemplated as she tried desperately to pinpoint the exact moment it all changed.

Samantha gently lifted her glass, swirled it slowly, hypnotically, then set it back down. She hardly noticed the handsome man seated to her right, watching every move she made. Samantha smiled before turning her focus back to her wine, to her journal and to thoughts of the conversation she'd just heard. How timely the topic of their apparent celebration. Was it a celebration of love? That seems oddly sadistic, given that the *"love"* of Carolina's life belonged to another woman. *Hmmmm!* But, on one hand it made perfect sense. Her husband had left her for someone new, perhaps regretting that choice now, so why shouldn't she gain some sort of satisfaction in taking something from someone else. Winner, loser, it's all fair right? She'd have to swirl that around a bit to fully embrace the answer.

"This love of ours, it's all a **dance**.

A **tango** of steps in to and out of

each other. Love me. Hate me.

Just don't let me go."

Florence, Italy

FRIDAY, MARCH 10, 2017

Deep in thought, considering all of the possibilities from her earlier eavesdropping fiasco, Samantha suddenly realized how much time had passed, noting that she hadn't thought about Michael's absence until now. She glanced at her watch, 6:00 p.m. Michael was late, but she couldn't have cared less. This, she knew was significant. More evidence of the road they currently traveled. Parallel, but not at all connected as it once was and, she believed, as it may never be again. Why now was it all coming to the proverbial head? Why was she so convinced that right now was the time to pull the trigger. Once the script in her head came to life, once the words left her lips, there would be no turning back. Was she finally ready for that? The conversation she'd overheard gave pause to the impulsive thought that yes, indeed she was. Now, just minutes after deciding that tonight was the night to set the record straight, she was not so sure at all — of anything.

She hated feeling victim to anything or anyone, especially a concept as elusive as that of being an *"empty-nester."*

It was so damned cliche, yet it seemed to have moved in and settled down in her life. Could all of her emotions and questions be explained away that simply — two words? No, she refused to believe it — the problems they faced now had been there all along, just hiding under the surface of their seemingly charmed life. They hadn't blindly wandered into this territory, she couldn't accept that. Surely there had not been one pivotal moment — but rather a lifetime together that changed the direction of their life, as a couple. What were once slightly bothersome habits turned into massive annoyances. The grating sound of each other's voices replaced the laughter and ease of their early days. Maybe those were the moments — the ones you ignore, blinded by the light of infatuation and fantasy. Maybe it's the fantasy that ultimately leaves you empty — not the departure of your children. Though she had to admit, their leaving provided the time and space to see it all more clearly — so differently.

"You're gonna crack that glass if you keep up the pace."

The man sitting next to her smiled as he cautioned her. She looked up at him, then down at the wine glass, just imaging how her thoughts had translated into physical action.

"Ha ha ha!"

Samantha let out a giggle, slightly flirtatious, if she were to be completely honest. He was, as she paid him more attention than when she sat down earlier, absolutely gorgeous. Deep brown eyes, black hair, curled up a bit at his collar, a familiar accent — Australian, she guessed.

"Ya know, it's just been one of those days!"

"Yeah I do know, but nothing a little wine and good Italian pasta can't help, right?"

He was cute and sexy she thought, wondering what his story was. What had brought him here, alone tonight. Curious, she turned to face him, her back to the door, taking her glass in hand, she smiled back.

"And a good laugh! Which I seem to have provided for you."

This was fun, and easy, something Samantha enjoyed, and welcomed. Where, she thought, had it all gone with Michael. They'd had it, for the better part of their marriage. But everything — conversations, laughter, sex, had all deteriorated these past few years. Now they were more often combative than comforting. It was a challenge for her to conjure up even the faintest memories of their early years together. She missed it and it saddened her to consider where they stood today. But now everything about her seemed to annoy him, and she was tired of it. Tired of trying so hard, to make him laugh, yell, cry, feel anything at all. Samantha sat there, mulling over their marriage. *It's too much effort,* she admitted to herself. *I miss me and I miss who I was with him, in the beginning. I can't remember the last time we laughed, I mean really laughed.* He used to say her dry wit and laughter were infectious. That's what he loved that about her, or at least he used to. So now, here's this guy, laughing with her and she liked it. *Michael,* she thought, *take your time, I'm doing just fine here, without you. Stay away.*

"So what brings you out tonight?" she asked boldly.

"I'm here for a couple of days, on my way back to Rome. I always have a good time here. Florence is easy, you know? Then tomorrow comes, and it's back to reality."

"Florence is my slice of heaven, my most perfect place. I come as often and stay as long as I possibly can."

"Sounds like you'd be a great tour guide." He paused, sweeping his hand over her shoulder. "Tomorrow?"

Shit, now what? He was responding to her energy which was most definitely inviting, but not at all genuine. She was hardly available to escort this guy though the city, tomorrow or any day soon.

"I'm not really available . . . "

He interrupted her, "Really? Come on, I'd love a real insider's view of Florence, it'll be fun."

Oh she had no doubt that it would be fun. More fun than she needed right now. And there it was, that voice, her voice, screaming at her, coming through loud and clear.

"No, I mean, I'm NOT AVAILABLE."

Her emphasis on the last two words, actually made him laugh.

"Relax, I'm just suggesting a city tour for the day, not a lifetime!"

Ha, knock out attempt in the first round. She took a moment before responding, turning her back to him, she looked past the crowded bar to the front door, still no Michael.

"What I meant was, I'm waiting for my husband just now and we are going to Venice tomorrow. Two nights, so if you're in town Monday, that could work."

Proud of how smoothly she recovered, Samantha silently

patted herself on the back, satisfied to think she could still banter with the best of them.

He reached over and laid his hand across her forearm, whew, the energy she felt! This guy could be trouble.

"I saw the ring, it's what took me so long to speak to you in the first place. I don't do married women."

Of course you do, she smirked to herself, *you're doing it right now and if I went along with this, we'd be headed back to your hotel, the penthouse no doubt, where you don't take married women.* She'd heard that exact line before, but she got it now. It's a game, one she used to know how to play, and one she found intriguing tonight, but it would have to wait. As these thoughts whirled, he reached in, hand firmly on her thigh, as he whispered, lips grazing her ear lobe.

"I think I'll stay through the weekend. Give it some thought, how you'd like to spend the day. I'll . . .

Just as that word left his lips, a familiar voice chimed in.

"Hey, babe, sorry I'm late." Michael always had impeccable timing, in business, in relationships, in love and tonight, no exception, was priceless!

Samantha scooted back on her stool and turned to face him. He had a curious look about him. Not angry, but he knew he'd walked in on something.

"Gonna hit the can, ask Lucca for my usual, thanks, Sam." He glared at the man seated next to her as he passed. This would be a conversation, no question but she'd be ready. He'd kept her waiting, more than an hour, fuck him. She can talk to whomever she liked and she would absolutely remind him of that.

"Your husband's here," he smiled. She was taken with

his easygoing charm. "Take my card, if he keeps you waiting again, call me."

And with that he was gone. Now Michael would return and it would begin, again. She looked toward the patio to see Stefania and Carlo walking in. *Thank God, what timing!* Samantha was relieved, social barriers in place, an argument would need to wait. Michael would not let loose in front of these two, not here anyway. Not tonight, they were out to celebrate their deal in the town of Sesto, the start of the "next big thing". All was good for the time being.

Samantha jumped from her seat, if only they knew how happy she was to see them just now.

"Ciao" Stefania greeted Samantha with kisses and hugs.

Huh, there it is again, Sam sniffed about, Grain de Soleil, faint, definitely not on Stefania, but hanging lightly in the air, across the bar. Samantha's head spiraled around, searching for Carolina and company. *How funny* she thought, *twice in one night. I need to pick some up tomorrow, I do like it.* She drifted momentarily back to her encounter, she'd have to look at his card, because she never did get his name. But one thing stuck, "then tomorrow comes," his words, echoing her mantra. It was at times a term of endearment between her and Michael, other times a reminder that tomorrow would come, and her actions today would have consequences. Funny that this stranger spoke the same words. Funny, not funny, happy, not happy; every aspect of tonight was at war. Conflict theater at its best, and she was the star. *Oh what this night will be.* Michael's warm yet sardonic embrace, as he kissed her cheek, jolted her back to the moment. *Yup, he has his armor up and he is ready for battle.*

"It's late, we should head over to the Excelsior soon."

Samantha wanted to get ahead of the night. They had 9:00 p.m. reservations, she didn't think she was being unreasonable.

"We've just ordered drinks, what's your rush?"

Michael's tone was forcibly pleasant, maybe not to Carlo and Stefania, but to Samantha his message was loud and clear. He'd be calling the shots tonight, for now anyway. She could let it go, she'd been to this dance before and they were both damned good at it.

"Of course, honey, I forgot, Lucca."

A cold smile tilted the corners of her lips. Just as the words left her mouth, Lucca, Caffe Rivoire's bartender extraordinaire and their long time friend, lined the bar to her left with cocktails for the group. Samantha winked at him, he knew all too well how to manage this foursome. Three Negroni's, his claim to fame, and an Amorone for her. *Okay,* Sam thought, tilting her head back to exhale her anxiety, *I can roll with this, for now. I want to have a fun night, it may be the last one for awhile.* She picked up the glass and offered a toast, "To friends, to progress, to life!"

Clinks, smiles, cheers and so it went. Stefania and Samantha caught up on family, the flight over, Stefania's plans to come to the states for Josh's graduation. While Michael and Carlo talked about the day's transactions and developments, Samantha felt comfortable and began to relax. Maybe the wine, maybe the jet lag, maybe the idea that she just wanted to have fun. To stop worrying about what was coming or what the world had in store for her. Being present in any moment was becoming increasingly difficult for her. She'd take this time and really enjoy it.

The friendship she shared with Stefania was different. It was an offspring of the relationships Michael, Carlo and Stefania had formed in college when they were all TCU undergrads. There was a part of Samantha that always felt like the outsider, a guest. In part because of the significant age difference, but mostly she viewed them as elite members in a very private club. One with such strong roots, memories, history, she often felt like she missed the punchline. She'd met Michael in Florence the summer after she graduated from USC, and had decided to return to Italy to work and vacation. He and Carlo already had an established and successful real estate partnership, seamlessly merging cultures, countries and families. They'd made incredible investments along the way as well, the benefits of which continued to roll in. Michael was originally from New York, and had stayed in Dallas after graduation, where the two worked, building their partnership across the continents. Carlo and Stefania married soon after graduation and the Dallas debutante settled in to her married and Italian social life with all the ease and grace you might expect from one with her pedigree. Her family was an old oil dynasty and she made no secret of her history. It wasn't that she flaunted her background, but she always made sure you knew exactly who you were dealing with. Somewhere along the line Stephanie became "Stefania", but Samantha never bought in to the adaptation, still calling her Stephanie. Maybe it bothered her, maybe not, she never let on one way or the other. One of the "southern girl" gifts of diplomacy that Samantha, a Southern California native, had never quite mastered.

Stefania was kind though, and they'd had a lot of fun over the years. But their friendship never evolved the way Samantha had hoped. She'd longed for something similar to what she shared with Kelly, and it disappointed her that it never materialized. And, if she were honest with herself, she'd have to acknowledge that her disappointment often fueled the fires of conflict between them. Samantha had tried desperately over the years — gifts, trips together, phone calls, constantly reaching out. But Stefania just never responded the way Samantha hoped she would. She took it personally that Stefania could be so caring and supportive of the women who made it in to her inner circle, but wouldn't accept her the same way. Over time, it turned into resentment, which she chose to bury. Ultimately, it brought them to the benign relationship they shared today. One of tolerance rather than love.

Maybe Stefania resented Samantha? Maybe Samantha was not at all the woman Stefania hoped Michael would bring into their lives. These questions plagued her for years, feeding her insecurities — the desperate need from her teen years to remain invisible. During her early years with Michael, Samantha brooded that she didn't measure up. Stefania's superficial relationship with her only made her more insecure. Fortunately, their separate lives on two different continents helped ease the sadness the emptiness of that relationship presented. The times they did get together were easy enough to get through without too much difficulty. Sharing life's milestones: business successes, failures, vacations, births, deaths. Samantha believed they had a special bond. Maybe one that just grows over time, based in familiarity more than genuine affection that would stand on its own. But the years had been good to them both and the foundation that only so many years and history can forge was one of the good things Samantha felt when she looked back over it all.

As Michael leaned in to kiss Samantha she caught an odd glance between him and Stefania. Strained, she thought and weird — *What was that about?* More of the TCU club private goings on that she never quite got? Maybe, but this was different. Samantha pulled back after allowing him a quick peck on the neck. She wanted to take immediate stock of what she'd just witnessed. He turned to continue talking with Carlo. Stefania didn't flinch but her eyes were burning through him. Sam's internal temperature began to rise, she was consumed with anger. *Okay, what the fuck is this?* Samantha nearly said out loud. *What am I missing here, there is definitely shit going down?*

"Stephanie," Samantha pulled her attention away from Michael, "are you okay? You seem upset?"

"Oh no darling, so, so tired. It's been a dreadfully long week, you know. Antonio just went back to Boston, finishing up this semester. So hard to believe he'll be graduating and heading out in to the real world! It was a fabulous visit, but having him home is always so tiring."

Stefania took a sip of her drink and laughed. It was fake, this much Samantha knew, Southern tact aside. Their son Antonio was handsome, brilliant, fun and easy to be around and Stefania was in heaven anytime he came home. This was not what was bothering her. There was much more to the story, Samantha was sure of it.

She decided she'd wait till dinner to push further. A few more cocktails might loosen Stefania's grip on keeping in what was really bothering her. But she just could not let go of the image — Stefania's stare was accusatory, sinister almost and so not like her. This was a woman who closely guarded every emotion. She was always charming and welcoming, to some appearing disingenuous. But Samantha had learned long ago, this was just who she was. There were many times she envied Stefania's grace under fire. That made her even more curious and uncomfortable about the interaction she'd just witnessed. So out of character, *damn,* Samantha conceded, *I gotta know what's up, there's no way I'll make it through till dinner.* She would wait and she would make it through, there were other more pressing matters at hand that needed her full attention.

Time passed quickly, liquor and laughter flowed freely. It was good, Samantha looked over, making eye contact with Michael, a maneuver they'd mastered over the years, letting the other know it was time to move on. Michael closed out the bill, they all said their goodbyes to Lucca and made their way onto the patio, heading through the now crowded Piazza della Signoria. Samantha would never tire of the continual ebb and flow of energy from residents and visitors. Each hour of the day brought a different crowd. Enchanting, she thought, how every soul there came for something, someone and they all seemed to leave fulfilled, taking a piece of the city with them when they left. She did, every time. The experiences, the memories filled her up, just enough to hold her over till her return. Florence was a drug for Samantha. One she took willingly, always hoping each time would be enough. It never was, she finally reconciled that, her cup would never really be full. She'd always leave a bit of her heart here and have to return to claim it. Only when she made it back here to the cobblestone streets of the old city, did she genuinely feel a sense of inner peace.

Michael took her hand as they walked. Stefania and Carlo were a few steps ahead. It felt good. He was strong, she'd always loved that about him. She felt safe, Michael would take care of her and their life would be perfect. That was her dream, a good one while it lasted. Funny, she thought, the fine line between love and hate. The very traits that draw you in, that capture your heart, they are the ones that end up doing the most damage. The ones you come to loathe, find intolerable and hate. *God that's harsh,* was she really there? Was hate now a part of the conversation? *How did we get here?* Samantha looked up at him wondering what he was thinking at this very moment. She really couldn't tell and that alone was disconcerting. His actions were warm, taking her hand, talking as they were, but something was off. Was he really still pissed over what he walked up to back at Rivoire? She was pretty sure that was not done, he would wait until they were back in the suite. Michael would never make a scene, he'd make her wait, worry about his response and then let it all fly privately, image intact. She was never that good at keeping her feelings in. Truth be told, if she'd walked up on him in the same situation, she'd have lashed out right then and there. That was the problem between them. Samantha was impetuous and impatient. If something was wrong or if she was upset, she'd need to make every attempt to right it as quickly as possible. Paying no mind to her surroundings, situation or consequences. Michael often argued that she was spoiled and immature, observations that infuriated her, fueling the arguments even more. She needed immediate resolve and that was not always possible, which of course made matters worse.

"Huh!" she finally said to him, "strange night isn't it?"

She looked up and directly into his hazel eyes, which changed hues and depth often, just as the world around him did. Tonight they were particularly golden — gorgeous — damn they could still melt her heart.

"What's that? You okay? You seem more jet-lagged than usual. Let's make it an early night. What time did you book the Venice train in the morning?

"8:30, we arrive at 10:35."

"Okay, good. I'm wiped too, ready to eat something and get back, relax, sleep!" Michael said with a laugh.

Well okay, she considered, *I'm just gonna roll with this, because none of it makes any sense right now.* She watched him, laughing as he strolled, knowing his body language was anything but relaxed. Stefania and Carlo glanced back to see that they were still behind them. Michael stepped ahead to talk to Carlo. Samantha kept her distance, falling deeply into her thoughts as she walked. *How? How?* she silently screamed, *did we end up here? Who the hell are we?*

"You took my **breath** away.

You stole my heart. To this day,

I chase the **memories**."

Florence, Italy

FRIDAY, MARCH 10, 2017

Samantha was acutely aware of the distance between them as she followed the three of them. *More space, more time,* she wanted that now — as the pressure and fears of the day closed in around her. She settled into a mindless rhythm, leaving just enough yardage to observe yet not so much that her distance appeared deliberate. The laughter from the trio drifted back to her in muffled, staccato breaks. Stefania, in the middle, linked their arms together as she led the way. Samantha watched Michael smoothly navigate the rutted cobblestone, the Arno river's breeze sending strands of his thick, wavy hair airborne. He was just so damned sexy, the years had been good to him. Smiling as she admired his profile, she drifted back to the summer of 1992, strolling arm in arm with him on this very road. A sweet taste of the memory settled on her lips. There was love in her heart still and the feeling was as warm as the air she breathed tonight.

The courtyard of the Ufizzi Gallery served as a venue for musicians, artists, street performers. Samantha loved it there and often found herself escaping inside the enormous plaza. The high arches and thick, porous walls leading out toward the river provided an acoustical dreamland. Artists attempted to preserve the scenes, sketching or painting every possible angle. But she considered the history and lives that once lived and walked across the courtyard to be sacred and any attempts at replicating them always fell short. Some things, she believed, were better left to one's own narrative. Stories that should be told from the genuine experience of sharing this magical space. Summer nights were alive with new talent and seasoned players out for the sheer enjoyment of sharing their art. Early in the evening on Monday, June 15 was no exception and a night Samantha would remember forever. She found comfort leaning against a pillar furthest away from the river, both to block the warm wind rising from the Arno and shield her pale blue eyes from the sun, lowering itself into position for another inspiring close to the day. The object of her affection that night was a violin and flute duo playing a Corelli piece she'd long adored. The young couple playing were so in touch with each other, perfect harmony it seemed musically and personally, she wondered if she'd ever find that connection. Music, especially from this time period, always swept her away. She was hopelessly infatuated with the notion of a life lived in another, more romantic period. So much so that she hadn't noticed the man who'd moved in next to her. He kept a respectful distance, at first, but as the music ended he took liberties with those boundaries. Samantha, dressed in a fitted black cotton sundress, had an air about her, casually elegant and confident. She was young, he noted, but there was a hint of maturity to her that intrigued and attracted him from the moment he laid eyes on her. Here was his shot, who was this adorable blonde, eyes welled with tears listening to student musicians, so genuinely moved by their performance. There was a story behind those sexy eyes and he wanted to know all of it. He leaned over, as she turned to leave, reaching out to her with a tissue. It startled Samantha, her thoughts lingering among the final notes being played, her imagination running wild with fantasies of what her life might have looked like had she been born in a different time.

"I'm sorry, didn't mean to scare you."

His voice was gentle and truly apologetic, she thought, as she took the tissue from him, embarrassed a bit that she hadn't noticed she'd been crying.

"Ha ha," she giggled, "I get so caught up in the music, I . . . I . . . don't kn . . . just lost you know?"

"I do." He answered, offering his other hand to her, "Michael. They were really good — nice music."

"Samantha," she replied, cautiously, scanning him while trying to remain polite and not too interested. Based on his response he was obviously not a musician, she smirked, 'at least he tried to be interested.' But inside, her heart raced, he was hot! Tall, handsome, athletic, 'damn hot,' she thought and she was interested. Ahhhh, summer nights, she loved the possibilities they offered and he was a possibility she would like to know better.

"Walk with me?" he asked, which she liked, no assumptions, not too arrogant, but sure enough of his game that he turned toward the river, extending his hand to escort her thorough the crowd. 'Yes,' she mused to herself, 'I will indeed walk with you.' As her thoughts steered her, she slid her hand into his and followed.

The sun, making its final descent, lit up the horizon, drawing upon all of the day's colors. Florence had that about her, she was rich and vibrant, arousing each and every one of the senses. She offered immeasurable joy to some, to others only pain, all the while craving your adoration. Florence could break your heart while whisking you away, along a narrow, pebbled path to salvation. She showed no tolerance for the faint of heart and that is perhaps what solidified Samantha's attachment to this city. Her actions surprised her a bit, as she ambled along, hand in hand with a man she didn't know. Not enough to warrant a turn around, or any hesitation for that matter. In fact, she felt an odd sense of knowing, a familiarity that warmed her heart, along with every muscle in her body. Had they met, she wondered? There was something about him — she was intrigued, and at that moment in her life it was all the permission she needed to follow this man to the river and anywhere else the night might take her. Crazy, she thought, but she belonged with him. His hand was persuasive and strong; she felt safe. It was natural and she liked that, her last few relationships had been anything but easy. Samantha longed for the connection and promise of love, of a future with someone, anyone, she was convinced that she may never find it. Of course, this idea was ridiculous given that she was just months in to the life of a 22- year-old college grad. Thinking that she was in despair and a failure in 'love' was laughable and she knew that. But her 22-year-old self was impatient, demanding and headstrong. She wanted it all and she wanted it now!

"Come on, we need to hurry if we want to catch the sunset. We can duck into one of the cafes up the road." Michael tugged on her arm to get her moving through the crowd. Florence in early

June was already rife with tourists, especially along the Arno as sunset approached. The spectacular display was one of the city's biggest attractions. For Samantha, it was all that and more.

"I'm with you, get moving!" She chortled and skipped ahead of him, taking the lead. They played this game of tug-of-war through the bustling crowd. Finally in front, Michael pulled her into a small cafe. He seemed to know it well, ushering her to a table near the window. A waiter followed, striking up conversation. 'Of course' she thought, 'ducking in here was no coincidence. Who are you, Michael?'

"Sam," he motioned to the view, "here is your sunset, no charge!" His smile took her breath away. 'Damn, who are you?' she asked herself as she looked away from him to capture the final moments of daylight and what she just knew was going to be an unforgettable night.

"Sam! Sam! Are you okay?"

Michael was next to her with his hand on her shoulder.

"What are you doing?" he asked, impatiently, which, in turn, annoyed the hell out of her. What she'd been "*doing*" was reliving the most perfect day she'd ever had, and she didn't want it to end. What a delightfully wicked state, she concluded, face-to-face with the man of her dreams, feeling so much better about life, viewing him in the rear view mirror.

"Um, I, I was daydreaming, sorry, caught up in some things I need to get done. You know me, forever making lists."

In the corner of her eye Samantha could see Stefania and Carlo in the doorway of the Excelsior. What, she wondered were they thinking? She had fallen quite a ways back without even noticing. At least she was on track to the destination, she repeated to herself again, *Oh what a night we shall have.* She pulled away from Michael and headed toward them, "I'm fine, let's go." Michael was perplexed by her reaction, but had his own 'lists' to contend with, falling in step behind her they made their way to the entrance. "Samantha," Stefania probed, "where were you darling — definitely not with us here." She smiled an almost accusatory grin and gripped Carlo's hand, turning to walk through the magnificent lobby to the elevator, and, Sam thought, *fuck, I need a drink.* Samantha still sensed tension between Stefania and Michael. They rode in silence to the rooftop, elevator discomfort at its best. Carlo, as often was the case, was on his phone, clueless or brilliantly ignoring the goings on under his nose. The kids used to take photos of Carlo on family trips, on his phone and label them as such with everyone getting a good laugh. Sam wondered how they'd kept it together all these years, studying both of them as the elevator doors opened. They seemed genuinely happy in their relationship, but Stefania was so different from Carlo, did she stay out of necessity — out of respect — out of love? *Is that all any of us ever do?* Sam wondered. It was hard to tell, neither of them were ever truly open with their emotions, so even if there were issues, Samantha would likely be among the last to know. *And,* she thought, *that's okay. I don't need to know their story, at least not every chapter.* SESTO was full, and she welcomed the distraction as the host, menus in hand, led them to their table.

"I don't need it." Michael abruptly nudged the menu.

Really? thought Samantha, *what is happening here?* As they sat down, Michael gave the host drink orders and turned to talk with Carlo — all but shutting out both Sam and Stefania. Samantha reached in her purse, checking her phone for messages and proceeded to bury herself in the menu. The whole situation was so awkward, she opted to tune it out, an exercise she'd mastered over the years, or perhaps a gift she was born with. Either way, it was a practice she relied on frequently in uncomfortable situations. She first noted its value as a young teenager when she believed blending into a crowd was her best shot at survival. As their waiter delivered their cocktails, Michael ordered an antipasti. He was agitated, that much was clear, but why? Samantha was in a bit of a tailspin, why was he so edgy? Did something happen between him and Carlo earlier, was there more to the new land deal than he'd shared?

"Stephanie, how was your day?" Samantha prodded, hoping to cut the tension as well as lead her down the path of divulgence. She failed miserably at both. "Oh, darling, you know me — always something going on." Stefania gave her a saccharine smile, pulling her napkin to her lips. "Some setbacks with my gala preparations. You'll be here for that, yes?"

"Not sure, Stephanie, what are the dates again?"

"September dear, I know I sent you the details."

Samantha wasn't sure where she'd be next week, much

less six months from then. "Of course, it just slipped my mind. Long day you know — I'm still on Dallas time."

Samantha laughed, trying to lighten the mood of the table. She glanced Michael's way, catching his eye, he smiled, taking her hand on his lap. It was warm, genuine, she thought, but still — something was just off with all of them, except of course Carlo. He rarely got flustered and was always off in his own universe. Maybe that's a good thing. She considered the roller coaster of the past five years. Passion has its pitfalls and she and Michael had certainly taken more wild rides than she'd ever imagined possible. Tonight was shaping up to be a very bumpy night. The image of Bette Davis saying those exact words in *All About Eve* made her laugh out loud. They all looked at her, Michael least amused of the trio, "Care to share?" he jabbed.

"Ha, just a funny thought, sorry . . . " Samantha was embarrassed, now more than ever. The waiter served the food but before he could leave Michael took hold of his forearm, "Bring us the check when you get a chance. Grazie." "Really, no dinner?" Samantha's question was directed to Michael, but Stefania quickly chimed in, "Sweetheart, we are so tired, I need an early night. I made reservations Tuesday night at Pinchiorri. We'll have a grand time when you get back from Venice. Everyone will be relaxed and rested. This is best, my dear."

What the hell? Samantha asked herself. *God, this night can't end soon enough.* And just like that, she got what she wished for. The waiter returned with the check. Michael took care of the bill and almost as quickly as they'd arrived, they were off. *One more shitty elevator ride to the lobby*, Samantha screamed to herself, but this time Michael and Stefania were not at odds as they had seemed earlier. Maybe they were all just exhausted and out of sync. Samantha's flight had been extraordinarily stressful and long, delayed leaving Dallas. Grateful, in retrospect, that Michael had insisted on sending their plane to pick her up in Rome. Though she'd protested at first, preferring train travel through the country, she was glad not to have to worry about connections and even longer delays. Perhaps the universe was taking care of business. She did need a good night's sleep. She did need to pack for Venice and she desperately wanted to talk to Kelly. All of it could wait till the morning. Their train was late enough that she needn't worry about any of it tonight. As she inhaled the fresh evening air, for the first time since landing Samantha could breathe, really breathe, she felt the city's energy envelop her and it was exhilarating. She always believed there were angels with her but never was it more apparent to her than during her time in Florence. The feeling escaped her up until this very minute, there they were on her shoulders, in her heart. She would be okay.

Then, as rapidly as she'd felt the earlier stress leave her body, it returned, most unwelcome, but there it was. There she was, yet again a bystander in her own life, observing — wondering — questioning. Finally, stopping dead in her tracks, Samantha watched closely as Stefania said goodbye to Michael, hugging him, she leaned in, her smile dripping with Southern charm, but nothing about her posture confirmed that this was a happy parting.

"Tell her — or I fucking will. Text me when you do," Stefania whispered in Michael's ear before sharply turning to leave with Carlo. *What the fuck is going on?* Samantha was more than curious now and would confront Michael directly on the walk home. Waves, air kisses, ciaos — blah — blah — blah. Neither couple, it seemed, could get on their way fast enough.

They walked, Michael turning the other way to leave his business partner and wife behind. Samantha slid her hand around Michael's as the St. Regis, across the way, caught her eye. The memories flooded in: holidays with the family when the kids were young- when they were happier. It had served them well over the years, she loved the proximity to the Arno. She paused to consider how fulfilled she did feel back then, her role happily defined and her focus mostly on raising the children. She knew she was blessed to be with them full-time. In this day and age it's a privilege, an exception. Michael had provided beautifully for them over the years. Of course there were economic ups and downs, but honestly they were one-percenters and she appreciated that accumulation of economic success. Panning the area connecting the two hotels, Samantha couldn't help but note the opposing forces at play right in front of her. The yesterdays on one side of the street, the todays and tomorrows on the other. The entire night was full of dissent, so many underlying currents at play. She'd evaluate that as well tonight.

She glanced back to see Stefania and Carlo in the distance.

"What are you doing, Stefania?" Carlo's tone was uncharacteristically stern. He'd watched her through the evening, the exchanges with Michael, her nervous behavior and he'd had enough. Carlo was somewhat of an introvert. He didn't engage in the drama Stefania thrived on creating in their life. Though he often appeared *"tuned out"*, it was simply that he had no interest in it. He enjoyed his life, his work and his marriage. Over the years he'd made a choice to ignore her incessant need to stir the pot. She was a good mother, wife and friend. Their relationship was mutually beneficial and enjoyable, though not the fantasy of romance and love he'd imagined in his youth.

Stefania's fantasy had materialized when Carlo, the young, handsome Italian exchange student, swept her off her feet and took her to Italy to build a life so far from Texas. For Carlo, it was admiration of her presumed independence and spunk. And here they were today, at odds. Why, he wasn't completely sure. What he was sure about was that she seemed to have taken on something that could wreak havoc on all of them and he was determined to stop her.

"Oh, Carlo, you're overreacting. You know how I value our friends. I'm just trying to keep everyone happy. And you, my love, look like you could use a gentle massage and a stiff drink!" And with that, she turned, taking his hand in hers to lead him home. Stefania was a master at changing the subject to suit her needs. As well as keeping Carlo content, anyway possible. For Stefania, it meant keeping up her charade and the appearance of a happy, loving family.

Michael picked up his pace leading them along the narrow streets back to the hotel. A long enough walk, Samantha calculated, to question him about the night without his being able to shut her down, yet not so long that she could paint herself into a corner by talking too much. She let him keep the lead, feeling connected but behind him, she could think more clearly. This would go one of two ways. She prayed for the second but envisioned the first as she silently rehearsed her opening lines. Head down, counting bricks, thinking of all the possible explanations, she noticed her phone light up from her purse. *Damn! How did I miss this?* Samantha looked at her phone in frustration. She'd missed a call from Kelly, and now a text:

"Sam, where the hell are you?! Listen to me — DO NOT SAY A FUCKING WORD. Nothing — do you hear me? Until we talk. Please, just this once, PATIENCE! Promise me — NOTHING. Call me as soon as possible. And tell that bastard I love him."

Smile, it was all Samantha could do as she tucked her phone away. Her sister had a way of making her want to laugh, even during the most miserable times. Funny and loving — always thinking of everyone but herself, that was Kelly's charm. Regardless of the situation, she'd end it on a high note. Out of tune and time as that may be, she'd never let a chance pass to let everyone in her life know how much they meant to her.

Okay, Samantha decided she would be strong and not discuss anything with Michael until she and Kelly spoke. Goddamnit, if Kelly was on point, it would require tremendous self restraint on her part not to talk to him tonight. She wouldn't be able to call Kelly till later tomorrow when they got to Venice. Patience, how she loathed that word sometimes. But she would question Michael about the night and what the hell was up between him and Stefania.

Breathe girl, you got this. She turned her attention down to her steps, once again. Pausing, knowing that once she spoke there may be no turning back.

"Michael? Are you okay?"

She led with the easiest opening, hoping that he'd spill it all of his own volition. Of course, she knew down deep, that was not likely.

"I'm fine, but tired. It's been a long few days. You? You seem out of sorts, what's up? There's more to it than your flight issues. You can play that game with them, but you know I always know when there's more. Don't be a bitch for the next three days making me wait for you to figure out how to tell me what's really eating at you."

He was flat with his response, emotionless. Samantha looked at him, unable to speak. How was it that he always turned it around, made any problem she had with him a problem she really had with herself. He was brilliant at this and if it weren't so damn frustrating she'd have more respect for the talent. But tonight she would follow Kelly's advice, patience. So no answer immediately. She ruminated on his words a long while before responding. His grip tightened in frustration with each passing second. *This is fun,* she mused, eyeing his discomfort. She was rarely in this particular driver's seat and she liked it. Michael wasn't a bully, but he had a way of shutting her down, making her question everything about herself and right now she felt nothing but empowered and it felt good — really good. A few more steps and she'd get to it.

"Michael," she began with a slow, deliberate pace, "I'm okay. What I'm not is this — I'm not going to let you turn my question about you into my problem. It's not my problem. I asked you because, based on your behavior this entire night, you are absolutely NOT OKAY and I want to know why." He opened his mouth to interrupt. "Please let me finish, Michael." Samantha spoke firmly over him, raising her voice slightly. A newer behavior for her, she generally acquiesced to Michael. He was the talker, the *"tour guide"* in their life. His demeanor was strong and forceful in its delivery and she'd always been okay with that position, but not now. "I want to know, damn it. What is going on between you and Stefania, are you having an affair?"

Fuck, she didn't want to go there straight out of the gate, not on the street anyway. But there it was, and there they were, in the middle of the old city, filled with passersby as she opened Pandora's Box. Actually, judging from Michael's reaction, it was more like she'd thrown it against the wall and it exploded. If there were ever a time her inner voice could have kept its damn mouth shut, this would have been it. But it didn't, she didn't and here they were, a standoff of sorts, Michael's eyes ablaze with anger and, as she looked more closely, fear. Something was terribly wrong, that much was clear. But she didn't know what and this was not the place to get the answers. She couldn't turn back, couldn't unsay what she'd just said. So she kept going, "Michael, please, what is it? I saw you and Stefania tonight, tell me."

Samantha pleaded with him, her approach softened once she looked into his eyes. She shook her head slightly, as if trying to help him get the words out.

"Sam, I am not having an affair with Stefania, I can promise you that. There is a lot going on and she has, as you know she likes to do, put herself right in the middle of what is none of her fucking business. Today ended well, but we nearly blew the deal. Carlo was so far off on the numbers, I don't know where his head was. We've got our work cut out for us this next week. I'm looking forward to getting to Venice. I'm so glad you're here, we need some time."

This was so not the reply she expected. Not the dialogue she'd prepared responses to. *Shit, now what?* Her thoughts raced. His entire demeanor changed in those moments and for that she was grateful. Worry took over and the thought that something could be really, really wrong turned her upside down.

"I'm glad to be here, Michael, this trip has been too long, too much time apart. Venice will be fun, I've let Allegra know our arrival time. She booked us at the Gritti."

"Good, good . . . " Michael's voice trailed off, as did his attention. He gazed off into the distance toward the Duomo, now shining brightly in the night sky. He knew this was one of the most beautiful sights for Samantha. She'd once shared that she imagined a princess in the tower watching over the city, protecting her. "Yeah, that all sounds good. Thanks for doing that."

They walked on silently, hand in hand, each wondering what the other was thinking. Neither of them willing to ask, not tonight. Tonight they would just walk, the moon chaperoning, lighting the way.

"Does seeking

relevance and attention,

even if it's not from you,

make me selfish?"

Florence, Italy

FRIDAY, MARCH 10 – SATURDAY, MARCH 11, 2017

The bright light of the moon's reflection jolted Samantha back to the present, and to the realization that Michael had not led her back to the hotel, but along the Arno to the back of the Uffizi. He stopped, turning in to her, wrapped his arms around her shoulders and kissed her. One of the long, sweet kisses they'd shared over the course of their life together. It was the one physical act they both embraced as theirs and theirs alone. Her lips, he'd often told her, were the perfect fit.

Michael gazed down at her as he lifted his head away, there was a story there, but he wasn't ready to tell it. He just stared at her.

"Michael," Samantha whispered.

"Shhhhh." He put his finger to her lips, "Listen, the river, the moon, do you remember?"

Did she remember? Of course she remembered! Their first night together, the sky, the lapping waters below, the kisses, the hopes that always come with the new. She had known from the first kiss that this would be different. The secluded corner table, window framing the Arno, chatting as if they'd known each other for years. He'd moved closer as the night progressed, emboldened by her interest. When he leaned in, hand on her shoulder touching his lips to hers so gently, kissing her, then tilting his head back, watching her response. Samantha knew instantly that this was not one to chalk up to experience. He had a commanding presence, empowered with confidence that perhaps only comes with age and experience, a trait she found intoxicating. No, she felt it deeply, to her very core, this was a connection from the universe and her life would never, ever be the same.

"I remember," she answered, a smile in her voice. "We were meant to meet that night, right here. Who'd have guessed it would take us for the ride we've had."

They both laughed, knowing each was feeling a touch from the same hand of fate. He kissed her again, interlacing his fingers through each of hers, leading them across the courtyard to the very column he'd found her propped against when he first laid eyes on her, and kissed her gently. She fell captive to his embrace and threw caution to the wind. They kissed, deeply, passionately, as if their lives depended on it. His grasp around her tightened, pulling her in, caressing her hair and her ass. She'd often joked about his moves, his ability to be in *"two places at once"*, always catching her off guard. Not that she ever complained, it was just one of the more charming aspects of their relationship. One she clung to now as she looked up and wondered where this was coming from, when did it all disappear? It had been ages since they'd touched like this, felt like this. Samantha was sure she was not alone in her questioning but thought best to let it be, at least for now. This felt so good, so right. Damn, Kelly, here you are again, in my head, knowing just what I need. Patience. Lay down the gun, don't pull the trigger.

They walked, quietly hand in hand, away from the plaza, away from the memories. She wanted to talk, not so much about the evening, her worries, but about her future, their future.

"Michael, I've been thinking a lot about what I might do now, with the kids gone, you're away so much, you know."

"What are you talking about, you keep things going at home. You hold it together. You ARE doing something, I need you there."

Michael's response was impatient. She knew the tone, it was dismissive, as it had so often been when she came to him with ideas of her own. How did he do this, admonishing her like a child, making her feel like one. *Goddamnit,* she thought, getting pissed off again, *I'm not going there with him. Not this time.*

"Michael, I'm not doing anything for me, and I need . . . "

He interrupted her again. "Sam, you're always off in ten thousand different directions, settle down, take care of what we need at home, there's plenty there to keep you busy. Why do you always do this, you're never . . . "

Michael stopped short, not saying what she knew he was thinking, *"you're never satisfied"*. It was his canned response to her when she wanted to do — be — see — more.

"Michael," she proceeded, determined but feeling so uneasy, hating that she was always afraid to talk to him,

"I've been looking into starting a blog. Lifestyle mostly, but from a landscape design perspective, you know, a chance to get back to what I know. Of course, the goal would be to moneti . . . ."

"Sam! Stop!"

Michael stopped walking, looking at her with his usual disapproving glare. "We have so much going on right now this is ridiculous, who's going to read it, how do you honestly think you're going to make money. Sweetheart, you haven't worked in years, you have no idea, it's a waste of time. You have work, for us, at home. We are in this together! Can you just be content, for once . . . "

Samantha didn't let him finish his sentence.

"No, Michael, I can't be. I'm not content, and we are most definitely NOT in this together. You're gone 80 percent of the time, the kids are gone for good. Of course I'm grateful for their journeys, I don't want them to come home, but I'm lonely, I don't know who the fuck I am anymore. I want to be relevant, I want to matter, I want to feel some . . . "

She struggled to find the words, and the strength for that matter to go on. Her voice was shaking, why was this so hard, she asked herself. Why couldn't she just say the words, tell him what she wanted, she was done being his trophy. She had a voice and she longed to hear it, to use it again. *For God's sake. When did that happen,* she wondered. When did she lose her voice? When did living become less about being alive and more about just surviving? Her life had taken on a monochromatic existence and she couldn't pin down a single event or moment in time when it all changed. It frustrated her, she wanted answers. She could blame it all on Michael, how much easier that would be, but it would be a lie. Somewhere along the way, she stopped trying too. What she couldn't wrap her head around was why and when exactly it all began and tonight that was pushing her over the edge. They were both at the dance, watching each other from opposite corners. Samantha often wanted to speak up, reach out, but rarely did, always letting it go, whatever "it" was at the moment. It was just easier that way. She hated the conflict, the possibilities that would inevitably arise from entering that arena. She'd reconciled years ago that feeling everything so deeply was both a blessing and a curse. It was a concept she could never quite handle, one that had her convinced if she ever said aloud what was in her head, her perfect little world would blow up. Even now, she found herself on the edge, ready to step back, walk away, let it go. She'd grown tired of this particular dance and she knew she couldn't give in, *please,* she begged herself, *don't do it. Speak* . . . and so she did; beginning with a whisper . . .

"Baby, I'm not asking your permission. I'm telling you, I have to do something, anything. I'm drowning here, don't you get it?"

Her voice quivered with the tears she was desperately holding back. Biting her lip, she turned and began walking, as she spoke. Michael followed reluctantly, giving her all of his attention.

"I don't know what the hell I'm doing," she continued, "I'm losing it, all of it. I have no idea who am I anymore, Michael. A mom, yes, but really that job is done. Your wife, hardly, you can't possibly deny that we've changed. We are so disconnected right now, you have to feel it too, be honest. Why can't you just support me? Why do you always put me down, you make me feel like I'm an idiot to even think I might be something on my own? Not without the almighty Michael paving the way."

Exaggerating her words with finger quotes, she was getting angrier with every word rapidly becoming tangled up in her emotions. She'd always been there for him, supporting everything he took on. And she did it without question, believing in him, in his vision for their life. Why was it so damned hard for him to extend the same blind faith? To believe that just maybe she could . . .

Her thoughts were interrupted as Michael abruptly pulled her to the right. They'd nearly missed the unobtrusive Borgo Pinti entrance to the Four Seasons, an irony not lost on her in this moment. She could hear her Mom, "Life happens quickly, if you blink you miss it all." Samantha considered that concept as she took hold of the brass handle, stepping across the diamond shaped white marble inlay that perfectly matched the bottom mahogany panels of each door. The glass door was heavy, swinging slowly as it trailed behind her. She closed her eyes . . .

A blink:

Mom was sick — then she was gone

A blink:

I was an adult — but I wasn't

A blink:

College, I moved to Florence

A blink:
I graduated
A blink:
I moved back to Florence
A blink:
I met and married Michael
A blink:
We had three beautiful children
A blink:
I lived the dream with Michael
A blink:
I survived cervical cancer
A blink:
I watched each of the children grow up and leave
A blink:
I wandered off into uncharted waters
A blink:
I woke up and wondered what the hell do I do now?

"The blinks — the what ifs — the what the fuck do I do nows"? This is where Samantha stood tonight, no closer to an answer, no closer to the truth. What did their future hold, where was it going, what did it all mean? *Fuck-Fuck-Fuck,* it was all she could say to herself, which was, on the surface, so ridiculously superficial. She knew that and she hated it, but more than anything, she hated where she found herself at this very moment, so unsure and out of control. The feeling sealed, profoundly so, as she listened to the loud thud of the door settling in to its resting place.

The lobby was busy, in the grand scheme of Italian life the night was young, just after 11:00 p.m. Nearly every sofa was full, voices filling the air around her, echoing off the marble floors, rising to the glass towering overhead, then circling back down, gripping her every breath. She was anxious and panning the lobby, its current occupants benign to her plight, only exacerbated the enormous sense of panic she felt coming on. Sam stopped, Michael kept moving ahead without noticing. Slowly turning 360 degrees, she needed to take it all in, appreciate where she was. *"Magic resides here,"* she'd once told a friend. *"She reveals herself the minute you open those imposing doors. If you give her your heart, she will lure you in and never let you go."* This was Samantha's explanation for the deep sense of belonging she felt each and every time she visited. The frescos, the columns, the arches leading to some varied version of paradise. The bright purple orchids between each sofa framed the magnificent marble sculpture. Every corner of the room had been so beautifully restored, reborn. The fifteenth-century palace's current incarnation was the most glorious hotel she'd ever seen. They'd traveled the world, stayed in the most elegant and luxurious hotels and resorts but this was by far her favorite and she wouldn't let the perplexities and uncertainties of her crumbling life detract from that.

Since its opening in 2008 it had been her home away from home and tonight, more than ever, she needed the warmth of its embrace. She paused, looked toward the sky pleading; feeling so much smaller than her five foot six inch, 115 pound frame, more vulnerable than she could ever remember; then she took the deepest breath she could manage. Her heart filled, she exhaled all the air that had been hovering just beneath the surface. The air she'd felt certain would choke her before the night's end.

Her head dropped, a sense of relief filled the now empty passageways in her chest. One foot in front of the other, Samantha made her way through the lobby and out the door toward La Villa and the Garden Suite. Michael was only a few yards ahead. She wondered about that, thinking she'd held back far longer than she actually had. All the while listening, as every step she took delivered a crushing blow to the tiny pebbles on the path to La Villa. The moon's luster clearing the way, she paid little attention to her direction. Michael stood at the suite's gated entrance, waiting, his arms raised and open. Samantha poured into him. The warmth of his body felt good, a stark reminder that she loved this man with all her heart — once. He kissed her forehead, leaning down on her as they walked through the door. The scent of orchids and fresh fruit filled the air. Michael turned to her, looking deeply into her eyes, though still not offering any indication of what he was thinking. He left her at the couch, opened the doors, and walked out on to the patio, the night air offering a warm welcome. The Garden Suite stood alone, away from the main buildings, beautifully secluded, one of its strongest appeals. The patio off the living room overlooked a private section of the gardens. Michael silently looked up at the sky, shadows from the moon still aglow.

Samantha stepped up behind him, wrapping one arm around his waist, handing him the scotch she'd just poured with the other. Fausto, their butler, had prepared the suite for their evening arrival. For Samantha, there simply was no better staff than those she'd encountered over the years here in Florence and tonight was no exception. The Eagles playing softly overhead, a bottle of Macallan 1824 Series 'M' Single Malt Scotch for Michael, Prosecco chilling for her, fresh fruit and chocolates. *Always the chocolates,* she smiled. Samantha craved the sweet indulgence, a ritual of sorts to bring closure to her day. Michael turned to her, looking deeply into her eyes, remaining curiously silent. He took a sip of his drink, set it down on the table, watching Sam as she lifted her glass. Still, without speaking, he ran his finger along her lips, at just the point where top met bottom. His touch was soft and inquisitive. Samantha responded, setting her glass next to his, pushing her chest into him. Letting her right hand drift down between his legs, she felt him responding as well. This, they were good at this, she thought as she slowly encircled the swelling mass, now fully present. Whatever else might have been going on between them, it would wait. His left hand cupped her breast, and she let out a moan, parting her lips, sucking his finger fully into her mouth. His body was warm and she was growing wetter by the second. *God how I love to fuck this man,* her thoughts now moving as rapidly as her breath as he pulled open her blouse, baring her breast for his lips. *How is it so easy,* she wondered, *we touch, we kiss and it's so fucking good, nothing else matters.*

The day behind her a blur, Samantha lifted Michael's head from her breast, took his hand and led him inside to the couch, pushing him down, kneeling between his legs. Watching him intently, she slowly unzipped his pants, exposing the rewards of her earlier efforts. He rested his head back, growing hard, ready for whatever she had planned. Samantha enjoyed this rare expulsion of power she held and she intended to use it exactly as she chose, watching him writhe with anticipation. She left her unbuttoned shirt on, loosely hanging from her petite, muscular frame. She gently swept into him, his pants floated to his ankles as she pulled aside his boxers, taking him in her hand, stroking and massaging to his sheer ecstasy. He tried to push her head down to take it into her mouth, but she resisted, taking pleasure as never before in making him wait. She kept one hand in, caressing him gently, allowing her other hand to cup his balls, her touch filling him with adrenaline. He pulled her up on top of him, taking her legs, wrapping them behind his waist. Her pants were still on, but he could feel how wet she'd gotten. He unzipped her jeans before lifting her up once more and slid them down her thighs. Samantha took the lead again, tonight this was her dance, she'd set the pace. She pulled back, dropping her black jeans to the floor. She knew he wanted that and she wasn't giving in to him, not yet at least. As they settled around her feet she slid back down his thighs and planted her lips on him. Wide open she took him in fully, reveling in his rapturous sighs. She sucked slowly, gently at first, progressing in her vigor as he got closer to orgasm, rubbing her chest on the inside of his thighs as she rocked back and forth leading him to a euphoric climax.

His body withered into the sofa, eyes closed, his hands lay on her shoulders. Samantha was content with her performance, she didn't want anything from him. As good as it felt when they began, her sense of where they were right then engulfed her. She couldn't quash the notion that he was hiding something from her. Then there was her part in it all, what she'd come here to tell him. When will it be the right time, she asked herself, when would she begin the conversation that could end everything she knew. She considered now, this instant, but she waited. She watched as he drifted into a shallow sleep, wondering, what did she have now, what did they have now? They had the dogs, five of them. She laughed, thinking about 'the canine factor'. A friend coined the perspective on life without the kids at home not long after Steven had left for college and Samantha's main companions were their dogs. *Are they enough to keep us together?* She wasn't so sure, but it was something to consider. What really bonds a family, a marriage? After tonight all Samantha knew was what she didn't know. She was no closer to answers than when she landed that morning. *Hmmmm, could that be were the truth is?* she asked herself. *The fact that I'm here, questioning our life together, maybe that's all there is. That's where the spotlight needs to shine. These are not the thoughts and actions of a happily married woman.* She'd heard that before too, it resonated more deeply now and she had to face the questions it raised. The volume of the voice in her head getting louder and more persistent: *The answers are here, and you don't like them.* Sam got up quietly, "Lyin' Eyes" came on. Glen Frey's haunting words followed her to the bedroom. Michael would join her there, she knew that, but he wouldn't wake her. This could all — this would all — wait till tomorrow comes.

"AHHHH . . . The secrets.

So damn many **secrets**.

They can set us free

or bury us."

Florence, Italy

SATURDAY, MARCH 11, 2017

Michael lay still, staring at the clock on the nightstand to his left, 1:32 a.m. He'd now watched the numbers advance, second by second for the last 62 minutes. The neon digits glaring at him, judging him. He was quite certain of that. "*How could you? Why did you?*" They whispered, quietly admonishing him for his behavior over the last eight months. *Stop it,* he shot back — to the clock — *you have no idea.* And he, now focusing in on the hour, had no more time. It was coming to a head, he'd played his hand and it was time to fold, before daybreak. This would no longer be his secret, but their story. And, he surmised in utter self-condemnation, theirs to decide on how the ending would be written. His eyes shifted to Sam, sound asleep, her back to him, oblivious to the storm about to hit. He watched her silhouette, envious of the calm, feeling his fears rise and fall in tandem with each breath she took. Catching the flash of light from his phone, he reached over, turning to block the obtrusion, so not to wake her. Another text, the fourth since his futile attempts at sleep had begun.

"Well? I'm telling her, you have to know this. I will not keep your secret Michael, I'm done here. Trust me, I will not be kind, sorry — too much damage. You fucking asshole. I don't care right now. But you, my darling, should care in spades."

He would have slammed the phone down, but he didn't want Sam awake — no, he needed time here. *Fuck!* He set the phone down next to the clock and turned to Sam. Watching her sleep, her tranquil, even breaths provided him a sense of peace, at least for the moment. *God you're beautiful*, he thought, struggling to remember the last time he'd looked at her — really looked at her in this way. How had he ended up here — where did she go — where did they go? There was no other way now, he had to tell her. Take what came and figure it out from there. She couldn't be that surprised, not really, they had been at odds for months, years more likely. He would hurt her and he hated that. He loved her, yes, so here he was, posturing deals with the devil for a way out. Maybe just a page of the story, not the whole damn sordid thing. Maybe if he waited till they return from Venice, he could negotiate a truce with Stefania for her silence. Maybe . . . *Fuck,* he repeated to himself. He knew there was only one way out as shitty as it would be. He needed to man-up and face it head on. He'd failed miserably. He'd failed his wife. He'd failed his children. He'd failed his friends. He'd failed himself. He gazed woefully out the open window, took several deep breaths, closed his eyes and slowly began stroking her arm . . .

"Sam, wake up babe."

Michael sat up nudging her to roll over to face him. She slowly opened her eyes, groggy—part alcohol—part dead sleep.

"What?"

She asked, secretly hoping he didn't want sex again, she just wanted to sleep. It took her a minute to grasp hold of her surroundings, she really had been in a deep sleep. Samantha felt the involuntary twitch of her neck, the aggravated wrinkle in her nose as she scanned the bedroom to see that there was nothing out of the ordinary. Then sitting up slightly, she leaned back onto her forearms, observing. The moon was bright, casting a shadow over him as he began to speak. Slowly at first then quickly, hardly stopping for air, it just poured out, he couldn't turn back — not now . . .

"I met someone, Sam, last summer. It's over now, but I needed you to hear it from me."

He stopped, not taking his eyes off of her, waiting for her to respond before he continued. She sat there, no words, no movement, eyes hardened on him. He waited, an eternity it seemed, until he couldn't wait any longer. "Sam! Say something! Please!"

Samantha was saying plenty, on the inside and she was quite sure she'd be better off if that's where it stayed. She looked into his eyes, deeper and deeper, stunned by his midnight revelation. This she had not seen coming — at all. Everything wrong with them right now, that he could have an affair didn't necessarily surprise her, but watching him, this was different. He hadn't just met a stranger and fucked her. That she could deal with, but this, this was more. Samantha knew that look in his eyes, she'd been on the receiving end of it; the surging emotional waves, wondering if you've met another soul you could spend your life loving. She'd been the recipient of his heart falling — the attention, the passion, all of it — a lifetime ago. How strange to see him wearing those emotions now, alive and new and for someone else. She didn't move, barely breathing, her eyes transfixed on him without change or hint of what she was telling herself, which was driving him insane. *What have you done, you bastard?* she asked herself. *Samantha, choose the next words out of your mouth very carefully.* Michael waited for her to respond, scream at him, hit him, cry — anything would be better than this. But Samantha kept still, watching him, a thousand and ten things running through her head in as many directions.

I hate you.

I love you.

How could you?

Why did you?

Why tell me?

Who are you?

Who is she?

Now what?

Samantha couldn't speak. The words clung to the roof of her mouth, unable to swallow, she tried to bring them to life — nothing. Her heart was racing at the speed of light, yet everything around her was moving in slow, agitated motion. The blood flowing through her veins began heating up, she could feel them expanding, ready and willing to suffocate her. *Is this a heart attack*? She questioned the possibility. Physically, no — emotionally, absolutely. Her heart was under attack, her soul ached, a scorching pain she had never imagined possible. Samantha felt numb at first, disconnected from her limbs, a visceral ripple of loss and contempt encroaching on every cell. Michael's betrayal was an attack on her, on their life. What could he possibly expect her response to be? She wrestled with that notion as she worked to fend off the anxiety rising within her.

Samantha kicked the down comforter off with her feet and rose to her knees, resting her bare ass on the backs of her ankles and stared down the man she'd given more than a quarter century to. The man who only now had decided to share that he'd been carrying on with God knows who, for God knows how long. *Why! Why now?* She asked herself, eyes piercing him with a frightening blend of hatred and fear and silence. It was the silence that was killing Michael at that very moment because this was not Samantha's reaction to things. She was impetuous, emotional, reactive. But this, this was chillingly different and for the first time Michael began to panic. He'd arrogantly assumed he knew what her response would be and therefore how to protect and save the relationship. He'd been gravely mistaken. He could sense, in her quiet, motionless resolve, that the pain his confession would cause her, could in fact be pain that they may never recover from. That their relationship may not be something to be salvaged. He wanted to force her to respond, but he knew better, he'd have to wait, much as that frustrated him. *Damn it, Sam,* he thought, his head exploding now, *please, talk to me.*

The day, the night, now this. In truth, part of her was pissed. She wanted to leave, she'd come here to tell him as much and here he was now telling her, he'd already left. He'd stolen her thunder. When, where, how often, the questions kept pouring in. Samantha looked away finally, to the open doors, out to the garden lit up fully now by the moon's glow, allowing the fountain's persistent flow to drown out the voices screaming in her head. None of it looked the same. In the seconds it took for him to utter his confession, to spew those three ugly words from his lips, the entire landscape of her life changed color, texture. It turned into an epic landslide brimming with dirty, jagged scraps of junk, a stench reeking of waste, the remnants of a marriage and a life. Her life — their life! As she studied the scenery beyond their seclusion she laughed to herself at the irony. Cautiously she turned back to face Michael head on. She carefully peeled her tongue from the roof of her mouth, using it to part her lips, licking them in search of moisture. Slowly she began to speak, listening to her voice, an echo, weak and unfamiliar . . .

"What? What are you saying? Michael? Wha . . . "

Her voice trailed, he tried to lay his hand on hers, she yanked it away. "Michael, what have you done?"

She wanted to say so much more, but her mind was reeling and she couldn't put it together the way she wanted to. Frustrated, she buried her head in her hands, hoping to gain some clarity.

"Sam, I love you, I can't stand this, I'm sorry, I'm sorry, I . . . "

She didn't let him finish, lifting her head, her eyes focused intently on his mouth as he stopped speaking.

"You're sorry? You're sorry? Ha! Yes, you are fucking sorry, a sorry fucking piece of shit."

She felt a power coming on, she knew she had to run with the momentum while it lasted, because it wouldn't.

"What do you mean, you 'met someone'?"

Air quotes accentuating her pain and her outrage.

"I meet people all the time, it doesn't mean I fuck 'em, or even worse . . . " She couldn't say it, she couldn't bring the words, *"fall in love with"* to life. Maybe if she never said them aloud, he'd have a plausible explanation for his behavior the last eight months. A convincing story to justify what he'd just spit out at her. She looked back out to the moon's shine, then down to the gardens, she was looking for comfort that didn't exist within those walls. The wind had picked up, weaving through the leaves of the trees in the distance, their branches groaning from the strain. She felt their agony, every ounce of her ached in harmony with the twists and turns of the wind's current. She didn't realize her body was actually swaying, shivering a bit from the cold breeze. Michael began to pull the comforter around her.

"Don't. Touch. Me."

Her words expelled a venomous charge, devoid of emotion, as her eyes bore into him. She raised her chin, studying him in the wake of her command. He dropped his head, lowering his gaze, following the lines of her body, as the duvet gently slipped through his fingers. This felt good to her, sardonically so. She was nude, fully exposed in every possible sense of the word and he had to look at her. He had to take stock of what was left of her right now, the physical remains of his wreckage. Fragments, she considered as she tried not to blink for fear of tears flooding through. Broken pieces, strewn across the bed in front of him. *Look at me,* she thought. *Look hard, look deep, but don't touch. Don't you fucking touch me.* Letting her eyelids drift downward and close, it hit her . . . she hated him — she really hated him. There it was, that word again, the one she'd admonished herself for earlier, with regard to the state of their relationship. And not because he'd cheated, but because, it appeared, he'd fallen in love. How perfectly it fit, how perfectly mad this whole thing was. How could he? It's one thing to talk about what would happen if either of them were to stray, as they often had over the years. They'd offer examples of what betrayals would be manageable throughout a lifetime together. Setting boundaries for what was acceptable and what was absolutely out of the question. Daring each other at times to cross the lines. Secretly hoping that neither would ever really engage in anything that might challenge their life together.

But here she was, looking their fractured promises in the eye and she had no idea which way to turn. Her first instinct was to run, run fast and run far. That was a natural reaction for Samantha when things got unbearable. She knew it made no sense here, not tonight anyway. Instead, she was fighting with herself. Fighting the urge to hit him, scream at him, get dressed, walk out the door and leave him. But, as she struggled for air, feeling the anxiety about to take over, she found herself fighting the urge to cry, to let him take her in his arms and make it all go away, make everything right again. All she wanted, when it was all said and done, was his love. Samantha's eyes opened, meeting Michael's and the tears flowed, uncontrollably. All that she'd held in the past few years came pouring out. Convulsive gasps for air, trying desperately to stop, she couldn't. It didn't matter what she'd been feeling these past months, today, or what Michael had just confessed, when she looked into his eyes, when she grasped the possibilities at hand she was heartbroken. She loved him and she was at a total loss as to what would come next. Michael pulled her into him, wrapping his arms around her, leaning his head onto her shoulder, crying with her. Trying to console her, lessen the blow of what he'd just told her, self-loathing consumed him.

"Sam, I love you. I love you. Please forgive me. Please."

He pleaded with her, hugging her more tightly with each word.

"I can't undo this, but you have to believe me, it's over . . . "

It's over, Samantha watched him say those two words, repeating them to herself. *You fucker.* And just like that, the bitter taste in her mouth returned. She felt nauseous, the mucky layers of his betrayal lay upon her, a weight she couldn't bear another minute.

"Let me go."

She needed a shower, she needed space to think. Steadily, she climbed over him and walked into the bathroom, closing and locking the door behind her. She braced herself against the cold wood, hands covering her face, then slowly sliding down to rest, prayer-like on her lips, thumbs holding her chin in place. She watched the empty, gray stranger in the mirror, as her ribcage collapsed with each breath. The tears returned, softly this time.

Samantha felt nothing, and yet felt everything. She moved to the shower turning it on as hard and hot and as she could bear. Slowly, the endless stream engulfed her, running down her body, consuming her tears as it swirled the drain, disappearing into the black hole. She watched for a bit, when pictures replaced the water trickling away. Images of their life, in no sequential order — one by one — memories, was that all they had now? *Is this our end?* she asked herself over and over. *Is this how it happens? We just say fuck it, life was good, now it's not — bye . . .* For all the contemplating she'd done, she'd never actually gotten beyond the illusion of a new beginning. Never really assessed how that would feel, how that all looked. *So thank you Michael,* she smirked, *thank you for doing it all for me. Thank you for meeting someone. Thank you for lying to me. Thank you for ending it. Oh, and thank you for telling me.* Her ire rose with each thought, she felt a deep sense of strength coming over her. She was in control of this, her actions now would decide the entire trajectory of their future. Her voice would matter. What did she want? How did she hope this would end? With these thoughts freshly churning, Samantha turned off the shower, stepped out onto the cold stone floor and wrapped herself in a towel. She stared at her reflection, massaging her aching head, then, pulling her fingers through her damp hair, she took a slow, long, deep breath, turned out the light, unlocked the door and walked out to Michael. Seeing the clock on his nightstand surprised her, 3:25 a.m., she'd been in the shower over an hour, not the few minutes she'd thought.

Clutching tightly to the towel she was wrapped in, Samantha took a seat next to Michael, on the edge of the bed, her leg touching him slightly.

"So here's the thing, I hate you, Michael." She shrugged her shoulders as the words slipped out. "Not so much because you cheated. I really do get that — we've been together a long time. So, yeah, I know it's unreasonable to think two people won't grow apart, feel different things, look for some excitement within the confines of a *"marriage"*. I get it, I believe it, and quite honestly I'm okay with that. What I don't understand is that you could let someone else in. You opened the door here — you didn't just have a fling — you had another life — for eight fucking months — you had a relationship."

Michael opened his mouth to speak, "No, no."

Samantha raised an admonishing finger up to the wind, "You don't get to talk here. You get to listen."

Lowering it to rest on her heart, she continued.

"You say it's over, how does that work exactly? You tell someone you've loved, someone who I imagine has loved you back, that it's done. If that's true, if you've ended your part in this, what makes you think she has? You can't just turn love on and off like that. At least I can't. And as much of a stranger as you feel to me right now, I know you can't either."

She wavered, her voice began to shake, determined not to give up here. She fought through and continued.

"You opened a door that you may never fully be able to close — what then? What happens to us — what's left of us?"

That was it, all she had, she burst into tears and laid herself across his chest.

Michael took Samantha into his arms and cradled her, burying his head into her neck as he pulled the comforter over her shoulders. She lay still, conscious of the warmth of his body — staring into the distance — towards nothing in particular — just away — wishing she could disappear. Wishing she could be anywhere but here, facing anything but this. Suddenly she was 13 again. Reliving the days of whispers and stares, sympathetic gestures toward her offering anything but comfort. She'd watch them as sadness filled their eyes, their body language was heavy and helpless and directed at her. Samantha had no idea how to reach out, how to respond to people who only wanted to provide her a source of comfort. What she really wanted was for them to ignore her, to let her be, let her find a way to get back to her version of normal. Before her mother's diagnosis. Before life took her by the hand and turned her world upside down. Now, here she was again, forced to deal with the turn of events in front of her. How should she respond? What should she do? She closed her eyes. All she really wanted to do in this moment was disappear, close the door and turn off the noise.

She'd have to talk to him, there'd be no escaping that now. As much as she hated him, what he'd done, she hated herself. She'd come to Florence this time with an agenda in hand. She thoroughly believed she was ready to tell him they were done. At the very least that they needed a separation. She thought she had considered every angle — *Ha!* she smiled, reminding herself, *of course Michael would throw a wrench in her plans. Of course, we will do things his way. Stop it,* she grew impatient with her whining. *Stop pretending none of this is your fault. Stop pretending none of this matters. What if he'd really left you, what then. What if he is still in love with this woman. What if. . . .* Sam stopped mid-thought.

What if the real question isn't where do we go from here, how do we say goodbye, but rather, how do we get back to where we began? She closed her eyes, pondering the concept. *Has our life gotten so predictable that the relationship itself is the casualty? Did we abandon our marriage, each other, all in the name of survival? Can we even get back to who we were before life had its way with us? Good God,* she thought, *nothing about this day is what it might have been.* The tears returned, she welcomed them, clamping her eyelids together, she nestled her head into her arm — and cried . . .

Michael laid back, gently rocking her. His heart broke, watching Sam writhing in torment. Anguish he'd caused, no disputing that, what he hadn't anticipated was the depth of the pain in her response. He had not come to this place on his own. Their marriage had changed, they'd reached this destination together, albeit separately. This act of simply going through the motions. Marriage is a partnership but they'd stopped working together years ago. He'd have to address this — they'd have to address it if they had any chance of repairing their relationship. Although he also wasn't so sure that was what Sam wanted. Most definitely not sure it was what he had in mind. He'd grown comfortable in the duality of his existence, self-indulgent as it was. What if he'd waited, not told her and let life take its course. He wondered about that, could he have prevented this heartbreak. What was going through her mind? He let her weep, exhausted, drifting in to sleep, he kept hold of her, a protective shield he reasoned, but knew the opening to Pandora's Box was only slightly ajar, they had so much more to consider. It could wait. It could always wait . . .

"How is it we have shared the
same space, the same **dreams?**
Yet here we are, completely out
of touch with each other."

Florence, Italy

SATURDAY, MARCH 11, 2017

Samantha lay still, wrapped in Michael's arms, reluctant to move. She didn't want to arouse him, but she had to get out from under his grip, out of his bed. Slowly, she slipped through his arms, gently laying them on top of the duvet. Swinging one leg at a time over the edge of the bed, quietly shifting her weight, her body followed, she picked up her robe from the chair and tiptoed into to the living room. No wonder she'd been so cold, he'd left the doors to the garden open when he came to bed. Samantha pulled her robe tightly around her, crossing her arms for warmth, annoyed at first, until reality overwhelmed her. This, in the grand scheme of her life, was nothing. The moon still offered a slight shine, just enough so she wouldn't need to turn on any lights. She sat down in the very place, on the very couch where she'd sucked him to ecstasy hours earlier. Then she poured a heavy glass of his Scotch, put her feet up on the table in front of her, grabbed a handful of dark chocolate covered almonds and leaned back to contemplate the last two hours and what her next moves would be.

Samantha lifted her head, raising the glass to her lips, laughing slightly. *These lips. The same lips that took you to heaven and back, right here, not so long ago.* She took a sip, swishing it about before swallowing. *These lips would rather chew you up and spit you out right now.* The cruel, raw clarity of Michael's betrayal was closing in on her, a vice around her head, her heart. The anger she hadn't been able to express directly was welling up inside her now, a veritable tsunami of emotion. *You mother fucker. You've done this to us. You crossed the line, you did what we said we'd never do. And now you want me to let it be. Understand you, forgive you.* "I feel so dirty right now. I hate you Michael, I hate you. I hate you." She was whispering to herself now, the words were too much to hold in any more. Samantha popped two almonds in her mouth, as she stared blankly through the open doors into the abyss that lay beyond. She was looking for answers, re-playing everything, grasping thin air it seemed, as she bared her soul to the universe. *Tell me what to do, help me . . .* Her eyes remained fixated on the garden. She let her mind wander, detached from her physical being. She pictured three doors in front of her — ornate, gold doors numbered one, two and three. "Pick one," she murmured sheepishly, "What do you want — do you dare?" Sam alternated the pattern of letting the chocolate melt in her mouth then grinding her teeth into the almond, shattering its core, quivering as the splintered remains slid down her throat. Finally washing them into oblivion with a long, slow swig. She continued this in a near hypnotic state . . .

'Waking up in a strange room, wrapped in the arms of a man you've just met, oh Samantha, what the hell have you done!' Her first thoughts as she snuck out of bed and over to the window, to watch the city below just waking for the day. Samantha was no virgin and no stranger to one — night indiscretions, though she had become far more scrupulous in the months since graduation. While she chastised her choices of the past 12 hours, she couldn't help the feeling of sheer euphoria as she peered down onto the Arno, inhaling its splendor. What an absolutely amazing view she had, not one she'd ever experienced. Then she turned and took in her surroundings. She'd not seen a suite quite like this before either. So even if this was just a one night thing, this was a hell of a way to enjoy it. She smiled at her resolve, content to justify her behavior. 'Why the hell not, I wasn't looking for this. It was fun. It's all good and he was really good!' She let out a chuckle, louder than she'd intended, waking Michael.

"Come here you . . . " He called out to her from the bed, she followed the echo of his voice into the bedroom, into his outstretched arms. He bounced her on top of him and hugged her tightly. This felt good, really good and, if she was completely honest with herself, really different. But she wasn't about to show her hand. She'd keep these feelings to herself for now. They kissed, her lips connecting with his, puzzle pieces, twisting, turning, sliding into to each other, locking into place. Was this how love started? There could be no denying his feelings. Their bodies swayed in unison, composing a melody neither could hear, but both felt to their core. Samantha's eyes had been closed, painfully so, squinting, she knew it and worried how unattractive that must look, the worry you feel in the early stages of a relationship. One eyelid at a time floated upward and opened,

allowing her to focus on Michael's eyes, which were now inches from hers. So close, she blinked to see more clearly. Michael was every contradiction she could imagine. Tall, athletic, strong, gorgeous hazel eyes with a glint of turquoise. Yet his face, his touch right now — so gentle, soft, caring. The fingers of his left hand parted her bangs, running his hand down her hairline to her neck, where his lips took over. Their syncopated breaths were the only audible sounds in the room. Slowly, harmoniously they rocked in each other's arms, needing only the warmth of a kiss. Two souls, newly connected, forever entangled. Samantha ran those words through her head as Michael pulled her closer and slid into her.

Her body felt alive, more alive than she'd ever dreamt possible. Samantha liked sex, she was open to it and with it. She didn't give her body freely, but she felt no contrition for the purely physical relationships she'd forged through her college years. She liked being close, but had no interest in commitment then. She often wondered if she'd ever let herself go, let herself fall in love, be contented with one man, take a relationship that seriously. But not all that often, she really was satisfied with her choices.

'Samantha . . . stop thinking . . . just stop . . . let go . . .' She did, for that moment, she let everything go. What was. What wasn't. She turned off the volume — the voice that offered her advice, admonishment, comfort, support — she could appraise all this later and knew she would. Over and over, regardless of how today ended. Her hands ran up both sides of Michael's frame, massaging his chest, moaning as she took all of him in her mouth and he exploded. She lifted her head slightly, looking to see his reaction to her; eyes closed, soft smile stretched across

his tan face. Inching upward, she lay her head on its side and drifted into sleep, their legs entwined, his hands resting on her so, so gently.

Michael sat down on the couch, next to Samantha, but she didn't move. He rested his right hand on hers, shoulders pressed into each other, but she didn't feel it. Her body was there, but her heart — her soul — they were wandering the streets of Florence in the summer of 1992, 25 years earlier, almost to the day. The day they met. The night that turned into the next day and almost every day after that. The day that set the course of their lives into motion. Their three incredible children. Success beyond anything either of them had imagined. Friendships, travels, holidays, memories — the memories that, brick by brick, had built the foundation of a life, of a family. The foundation that she felt crumbling beneath her.

"Do you remember the first time we stayed in this suite?" Michael asked. Samantha finally whispered, but she never altered her her gaze through the open door, out to the garden. "June 2008, we were the first to stay in this suite. The kids loved having us so far away from them, feeling *"so grown-up"*. We've done a lot of living here — you and I. Memories . . . ." Sam's voice trailed off barely audible. Michael squeezed her hand, she let him, still intently focused on the grounds beyond.

"Sam, talk to me. What do you want to know?"

Outwardly, his pleas were soft and sympathetic. Inside, the weight of his heart was suffocating. He needed her to talk, tell him what she was really feeling. This had never been easy for Samantha, she kept everything inside. Protecting herself, always fearful that if she ever shared all she thought, all she felt, no one would totally understand her and she'd be left with nothing but the endless loop of emotions and ideas playing to an audience of one. As much as Michael had tried to oblige her sensitivities over the years, he needed her to open up. Here. Now.

"I'll tell you anything, everything you want to know. You've got to talk to me."

Samantha remained silent for what seemed an eternity. Part par for the course, part wanting to make him squirm, to experience as much pain as she could inflict on him right now, short of a physical affront. Her entire being was numb. She turned her attention to Michael, moving only her eyes, so not to alert him to her changing focus.

"I don't know what I want you to tell me, Michael."

She really didn't know how to answer him, but she knew she had to start somewhere. She had to get this out of her head, lighten her heart.

"I want details, all of them. But really, I'm not sure I want to know all the hows, the whens, the whys. If I just imagine it all, it's less real. I don't know that I want you to confirm any of it for me, besides what you've already dumped in my lap."

Michael, started to speak, her hand gripped his and she interrupted.

"Actually, wait . . . tell me this Michael, why tell me at

all? Suddenly a conscience? You need to *"come clean"* with me? I need to hear it from you? Why?"

With that she lifted her hand, using it to turn his face into hers — inches away, she wanted to look deeply into his eyes as he answered. *No escaping now big boy,* she thought, *you want me to talk, here I am, fucking answer me. Now.*

"I've ended the relationship, I never wanted you to hear about it from someone else, I wanted to tell you so we could figure out where we go from here. Just the two of us."

He tried to lower his head and pull away, but she tightened her hold on his jaw to keep his eye contact on her.

"I love you, Sam. I fucked up, completely fucked up. There's been an ocean between us for months, you know it, regardless of what you won't talk about. We haven't been there for each other, with each other for God's sake. Do you honestly . . . "

And with that she cut him off, she couldn't take anymore.

"Shut up! Just shut up!" she screamed at him. "Don't. Not yet, you don't get to blame me for your fuck up. You made a choice, you had an option and I'm guessing your cock won. You and your damned ego. Oh poor me, Sam hasn't been there, Sam is this, Sam isn't that. Go fuck yourself, and the cunt you've entertained for the last eight months."

Her anger, fear and guilt of her own seeped in, knowing what she'd planned to present to him on this trip. Yet her newly found voice shrieked on. "Tell me, was it her platinum pussy, world-class blow jobs — or did she just stroke your ego, you never get enough of that, do you."

"Sam! Are you kidding me? MY ego? You barely make

it through a day without making sure I know how people love you, need you, want you. You make me feel . . . "

"Feel what Michael, incompetent, worthless, invisible? No that's how I feel. You indignant bastard — I need the accolades? You drink in every compliment, echo every praise laid upon you — it's a drug to you. You always make sure everyone knows how you've created us, our life, me."

Samantha was on a roll, standing up to face him, she stepped between his legs to fortify her position.

"I've spent so much of our marriage in darkness — eclipsed by your insatiable need to be admired. How you love to tell people that I was so young when we met, so "*not ready for prime time*". What the fuck does that mean anyway? Like you were so sophisticated and "*all that*" when we met!"

"Ha! Really, Sam? You have minimized every accomplishment I've made — somehow, it's no big deal to you that I built, from nothing, and sold our first company which not only gave us insane financial success but all the perks you've had no problem luxuriating in for the past decade. Your entitled arrogance blows my mind. I have the ego? Fuck you!"

Michael had never expressed his resentments this way. He'd chosen to keep moving forward, to ignore how belittled he'd felt over the years, how deeply he believed she just took it all for granted, that he owed her this life. "You know, maybe that was part of it, she actually respected all I've accomplished, you just expect it. You assume that the money, the status will always be there for you."

"Oh don't even bring her up like that. *"Respected"*, kiss my ass. If she respected you, she'd have said no from the beginning, you're a married man. You have a family."

Samantha didn't want to hear anything about "*her*" right now, she needed this woman to remain faceless, heartless, not a living, breathing soul who almost stole her life right out from under her.

"Sam, admit it. You wanted me to spend more time here. You liked us living separate lives. What did you honestly think would come from that? I'm not blaming you — not in any imaginable way. I'll own it. But it didn't just happen. Someone can't just come in and disrupt a life. A happily married life doesn't have the room or the want. We weren't that, we haven't been that since Ashley left for college."

"Ahhhh, poor Michael, not enough attention?"

Sarcasm, her downfall when she was hurt, oozed from every pore onto Michael, the rancor like a thick tar.

"Hmmm, let me think — oh that's right, same year I spent most of my time in and out of the hospital. Remember, the cancer? It was devastating, you remember that right? I assume, you remember — though you were here mostly, prettier views, yes? You did tell me you'd be lost without me, I do remember that."

Samantha stopped talking, that was painful, and wrong. She knew how he'd agonized over the news. The only blessing, an early stage diagnosis and likely no recurrence or residual effects. He had been there for her. She watched him wince as the words slid from her lips. She'd dug low enough, too low, even from her vantage point of his betrayal.

"I didn't mean that. I need to stop talking, we need to . . . " As Samantha continued, Michael took both of her hands into his and pulled her in to him.

"No, you did, I get that. I also know you didn't mean it the way it came out. I'm sorry, Sam. I can't stand this, watching you like this. But it is good to hear you tell me what's really going on in that head of yours."

He smiled as he spoke and she couldn't help but laugh. It was true, she never got to the heart of an issue in the midst of a conversation. She'd need to listen, take mental notes, obsessively brood for days, then reconstruct the original conflict and hit him with it all. An explosion, usually ignited by completely unrelated events. It was a protective coat she wore with little pride and immense frustration. Samantha wanted so much to be that girl who could easily speak her mind. Articulate her most private thoughts as well as her most strongly held opinions. She'd always wrestled with it, shy to a certain extent, never wanting to be the first to speak up, then waiting too long for her input to be relevant. She held layered, in-depth conversations with herself, covering every possible angle, responding to all potential rebuttals. But when the time came to have the conversations, ask the questions, give the answers, she held back, watching, listening, waiting — always waiting. Just long enough, she guessed, to see that she'd been right, if only she'd spoken up. She'd long admired that Michael could talk to anyone, anytime, about anything. He had an uncanny ability to get to the center of an issue and hash it out, covering every angle, answering every question, usually spot on the first go-round. She envied that, hoping someday to take on some of those characteristics. But they'd both become accustomed to each other's behaviors and fell prey to familiarity.

Hmmmm, she looked at him now, his breathing shallow but slow. *How do you do it?* She hovered forward and kissed him. In that instant she was consumed with hate and love. He'd just ripped her heart to pieces and shattered her trust. She hated his deception. Yet, as her lips merged with his, she was consumed with an unfettered physical pull, love, pure and simple. She loved him. How much, why and where it should take her from here, she had no idea. For now, just to be was enough. *Be here, be free; be you, Samantha, be you for once in your life.* Their kisses deepened as the sun was began to find its way into the morning sky.

The alarm buzzer intruded — shattering their calm. She'd set it for 5:00 a.m. to allow ample time to pack and make their 8:30 a.m. train. Michael cradled her into his lap as he stood, carrying her into the bedroom. First shutting off the blaring alarm, then laying her across the bed. He lay down next to her, both on their backs, holding hands, staring at the ceiling, unsure of how to proceed. Two awkward teens about to make love for the first time. To a certain extent it was the first time — for both of them, they were strangers, each fighting their own battles, searching for answers, yet willing to push the pause button and get lost in each other. *Maybe best,* she thought, *get lost in this, tuck these past few hours away. It'll all look differently in the daylight. I'll figure it out then. But for now . . . For now . . .*

"Song?"

Michael's voice snapped Samantha from her trance.

Perfect! she thought. Not only had Michael mastered the art of getting her out of her shell and the moods that often enveloped her over the years, but he had the impeccable gift of drawing on whatever experience fit the moment, completely changing the tone of a conversation or conflict. She thought back to how the habit had begun, while flipping through her mental playlist to answer him. It was during their early days, when love was playful and they were tracing each other's lives, past and present to get to know each other. Michael, tuned in to her musical passions, would challenge her to pick the song that fit the moment. Samantha believed there were lyrics for every situation she'd ever encountered and told him as much. Eventually, she turned it around and Michael began to search for the deeper meanings behind the songs he loved. As days turned into years, they found themselves using the game to get beyond the facade of an ideal life. Samantha had quit trying of late because Michael had become unresponsive. She watched the memories slip into darkness as she felt she'd done with so much of their life these past months. Michael used the challenge often, to try and get to her core, to understand what she wasn't saying. Both feeling powerless to shift the course they were on.

"Skies the Limit," Samantha finally answered, her upward stare remaining unchanged. She knew how this would hit him between the eyes, straight to heart. There were so many others, more fitting for where they lay this morning, but the impact of this would burn through his soul, which was her intent. Fleetwood Mac and Stevie Nicks were her go-to songs. She'd shared the lyrics with him during their first weeks. It would transport him back to the beginning — to the girl he'd fallen head over heels for — to the memory of who they were once. And, if she calculated the situation right, to his desperate need to win her back.

Samantha turned, looking through him more so than at him, to see his eyes full, tears streaming down his face.

"You?"

She asked, closing her eyes to wait for his answer.

"I Can't Tell You Why," he whispered, stepping over her one word question. Samantha knew exactly what song he'd pick and why. She understood his internal struggle, more than he could possibly know. She empathized with the self-loathing consuming him. The agonizing realization that the person who was once the love of your life might be someone you don't even want in your life. That maybe you'd given all you could give to each other and the best you could do now was to offer each other a way out, a chance to start anew. Sam opened her eyes, wiping away the tears streaming down his face. *Oh Michael, what have you done? What have we done to us?* she wanted to ask him, but she wouldn't, not now. So she made the first move, sliding onto him, shedding her robe in the process. One hand under his back, she pushed down on him, feeling him expand, wanting her. Funny thing about ego, as pissed and hurt as she was, she desperately needed him to want her, need her, pick her. Why work so hard, now to lay claim to him, to take him back. This was ridiculous, she absolutely understood that, but emotions, self-worth, every psychological profile she could imagine meant nothing. Her adolescent yearnings annoyed her, but they persisted as she massaged his ass knowing full well that he'd respond, unable to resist her advances. She needed to win this battle. How could there possibly be another woman, more attractive, sexy, and fun than her? She would not leave this country letting another woman, likely some 30-something tramp move in to her life. *Yup, this is mine, you are mine,* she concluded. *Fuck that bitch, she can't have my life. I get to decide when it's over.* And with that she slid him into her, sitting up, watching his every move as she took him to the edge of ecstasy. But Michael was equally driven to control their dance here, flipping her on her back, mounting her, pulling her legs up and around his neck, he drove into her hard and fast. Climax came quickly, an eruption of raw, seductive, physical and emotional release. She pushed off of him, lying on her back. They lay still and silent until the alarm sounded off again. A blasting reminder that Venice was waiting. A trip Samantha had planned a lifetime ago it seemed, before Michael had fractured their foundation.

"I'll be ready in ten."

Samantha got up from the bed and went into the shower. Another cleansing, this time to prepare herself for what would likely be 48 hours of hell. She couldn't imagine being with Allegra and not breaking down. Allegra had been a friend, family to Samantha since her days in college. She was older than Michael and wise beyond those years. She'd always been there, a mother to her in so many ways. There was no way Samantha could conceal her pain, but she wasn't sure she wanted to share it with anyone yet. She had so much to sift through. The warm water poured over her, once again washing her stream of tears down the drain.

"Michael?" Samantha called out to him, "my robe please."

Leaving the door ajar, he tossed it in to her. They passed each other as she came out and he headed in.

"Sam, remind me again why we aren't taking the plane? We are rushing to make this train when our pilot is sitting in wait for my call. Why do you insist . . . "

"Because I like it. Reason enough. A trip through the countryside will do us both some good. I'll be ready when you come out. Fausto has the car ready to take us to the station."

She turned away and started dressing, newly empowered, though she wasn't sure why. She knew he'd object to her booking the train to Venice. It was probably why she did it. Partly she wanted to annoy him, make him uncomfortable. She was the one who'd planned to drop the bombshell when she booked the trip. Her state of mind had been self-serving and self-protective. She wanted to be in the driver's seat and this was one way to achieve that. Michael loved his plane, but he hated the train, and that was all the motivation she needed.

Michael shook his head. Still aggravated, he left the room, showered, and quickly dressed. They moved about the suite in silence. Fausto rang the doorbell, gathered up their luggage and they were off. As if it were just another day, another trip. *Another life,* Samantha considered. *This could be any other time, any other place, any other man. What could that feel like?* She had a lot of thinking to do, and still needed to talk to Kelly who would be expecting her call this morning. *Jesus, she won't be expecting this turn of events.* Samantha would call her as soon as she had some alone time. She needed her sister today. They pulled up to the Santa Maria Novella station and walked to the board the train. She couldn't get settled fast enough. Michael, seated across from her would fall asleep shortly, and she welcomed the space it would offer her. Her own air to breathe, time to think. Riding the train through Italy was as close to heaven as she thought she might ever get. Earbuds in, music drowned out her inner voice. The voice she didn't want to listen to right now. She needed to clear her head, free herself from the admonishments, the questions, the scenarios that were determined to play over and over. She leaned her head against the window and settled back into her seat, drawing her knees up into her chest. She closed her eyes briefly, *check out baby, let it be.* "Edge of Seventeen" launched her playlist, Samantha peered out the window as the train pulled from the station. She was on the edge, not of seventeen, but of reason. Two choices as she saw it then. Forgive him, take him back, try to fix the many wrongs they dealt each other. Or, leave him, what she'd thought she had come to Florence to do 24 hours ago. Now, in the face of his confession that didn't feel right at all. If she told him she wanted to leave, he'd believe it was his affair that drove her away. If she stayed, and stayed silent, he'd believe she'd given him another chance. A chance to be a better husband, a chance to make their marriage stronger. These were not choices she'd anticipated having to make here. Now she had two hours to consider what to do with 25 years and what the coming years might look like. *That works,* she laughed to herself, smiling as the train carried them over the rolling Tuscan hills.

"You've always been my **kryptonite**!

My greatest strength, my greatest

weakness."

Venice, Italy

SATURDAY, MARCH 11 – SUNDAY, MARCH 12, 2017

They arrived in Venice on schedule and settled into their suite at the Gritti Palace. Exhausted, Samantha fell into a deep sleep after unpacking. Michael woke her up gently. Kisses on her forehead, fingertips parting her hair, the warm air rising from the canal below, all of it aroused Samantha. Michael was sitting on the bed next to her. She followed his gaze as she opened her eyes, out across the Canal to the angel spinning in agitation, seeking a stopping point, a direction. It seemed telling, Sam thought as she studied his watchful eyes, his head swaying with every turn the angel made. The two of them, she believed, in search of direction, meaning, something their life together to this day had taken from them. How long, she wondered, and as if reading her mind, Michael asked, "You slept a good three hours baby. How do you feel?" He was genuinely concerned for her well-being as much as he was dipping his toes into her emotional waters. Had the nap carried her further away or back to him?

"I'm good."

Samantha shook her head slightly, waving off the groggy air surrounding her. She'd answered quickly and honestly, but reality began to settle in, Michael's solicitous presence last night and this afternoon. Just like that, it all came roaring back — she wasn't.

"Definitely needed the sleep. You?"

"I slept, not as long, I'm okay. What time are we meeting Allegra?"

"At 7:00. Quiet dinner, she said, just the three of us, it'll be nice."

That would be nice, Michael thought, but he knew it wouldn't be just the three of them. Allegra's *"quiet evenings"* always turned into a spectacle of some sort. Samantha met Allegra during her junior year studies in Florence. She'd never admit to her exact age, just that she'd lived through most of the twentieth-century unscathed. Samantha had guessed she was about her Mom's age, which established the course of their relationship as the years passed. Allegra descended from Northern Italian aristocracy, the sole remaining heir to one of the most powerful families in Italy, dating back to the Medici era. She'd never married, a choice she claimed had been hers, always. Allegra was fiercely independent, charming, and a bit crazy, in Michael's opinion. Though Samantha preferred to describe her as eccentric, full of life. All true, Michael concurred on more than one occasion, when they argued about her influence over Samantha, who idolized Allegra, and looked to her for guidance through every milestone she reached. Allegra had never been married, she'd entertained several lovers over the years, had no children, nor discipline in every day living. Her *"examples'* made Michael uneasy, believing they may not always be the best example for Samantha, or any young woman for that matter, a dubious role model to be sure. But he kept those concerns to himself, broaching the subject wouldn't change anything. Allegra was everything to her.

Her *"place"* in the city was a fifteenth-century palazzo overlooking the Grand Canal, not far from Piazza San Marco. She had a home outside Florence adjacent to the castle where the Pazzi family is said to have conspired to overthrow the Medici family. The history and romanticism was not lost on Samantha, who'd spent her childhood fantasizing that she'd lived in that time. It explained her infatuation with the country and culture. Allegra also enjoyed an expansive villa and land on the southern coast, outside Positano. Tonight, Michael thought, would be a grand diversion from the past 12 hours, but one that he feared would lead them both further down the rabbit hole, especially when Allegra got wind of what he'd done to Sam. He knew full well that Sam would tell her everything and seek her advice on how to proceed with her life, their life. That aggravated him more than anything. What the hell could Allegra possibly know about a marriage, family, betrayal, commitment, love? Allegra and Kelly, *Good God*, he thought, that Sam had survived as she had all these years with those two holding the reins was nothing short of a miracle. His blood began to boil as he considered the possibilities of the night. Samantha sensed a change in him, his hand still on her forehead tensed notably.

"Are you okay?"

"I am, sorry," he moved his hand to her shoulder. "No I'm not, we're not, not at all, I hate this, I hate myself, Sam."

"Michael, please don't do this, not right now. Why don't you go down to the gym, get in a good run before dinner. I'm gonna go take a walk. It's gorgeous out right now. I'll be back in an hour or so."

She paused, choosing her words carefully.

"You can take this with you . . . I do love you, Michael. I have no idea what that means right now, or where it will take us, but I do."

He didn't care what it meant right then, he'd take it. He'd take any of it, a hopeful sign that maybe he hadn't pushed her completely over the edge. That maybe she'd give him another chance. He leaned in and kissed her, stopping to search her eyes. She was curiously calm, he chose to believe that it was a good thing. He got up, changed, waited for her to join him and they headed downstairs together. The elevator ride was slow and quiet, the air rose between the two of them, filling the small car with 25 years of feelings, thoughts, dreams, fears — words unspoken. Their eyes darted about, on the descending numbers illuminating above them, to the ceiling, to the floor, looking toward anything and everything but each other. Michael walked her through the lobby, kissing her cheek before heading to the gym. He wasn't sure where she was going, in any sense of the word. He just prayed she'd come back to him, for him, for them.

Samantha turned, away from the Canal, heading up Campo del Traghetto toward Piazza San Marco. She walked with purpose, past luxury shops and cafes that beckoned and had won her over through the years. She'd wanted time to herself, to enjoy the early spring afternoon, that much was true, but she also wanted to get to Fabriano. The stationary boutique opened in 2002, but the family became synonymous with making the finest quality paper during the thirteenth-century. Samantha fell in love with the journal collections instantly and, as the three full safe deposit boxes at the Four Seasons would confirm, filled their pages frequently, stopping in or ordering them for delivery to Florence so she could continue recording her every thought. It was late, they'd be closing soon, so she rushed, making the ten minute walk across waterways and through the old city, in five. Selecting seven new volumes was easy, the new bindings were magnificently embossed leather. Sturdy, simple, dependable, she observed, unlike anything she was presently facing. She proudly gathered her treasures, tucking them into her tote. She'd made it to the shop with ample time to make her purchase and still had plenty left before needing to get back to Michael. Mission accomplished, she smiled, waving goodbye to the shop clerk, giddy, almost skipping down the road, she opted to detour through the Square. The rising afternoon tide sloshed in unison with her steps.

"Venice is a grid of organized chaos," Allegra's words rang through her, *"walk everywhere and go nowhere, but you'll always end up exactly where you need to be, it's the beauty of this city. Don't weigh yourself down with a map. Let your heart take you where it wants to go. Follow the ebb and flow of the waters."* Where her heart wants to go, now there was some food for thought. She wondered if she'd ever really know the answer to that. Her heart had become a mosaic of every

fractured piece of her life up to that minute. She stopped, startled upon seeing her reflection in the window. Panning the silhouette, head to toe, she didn't recognize the girl peering back at her. She'd dressed in the first thing she could grab quickly, while trying to get out of the room. Distressed cutoff denim shorts, a lightweight, boxy, black, v-neck pullover, black lace espadrilles and turquoise mirrored Ray Bans. Her tousled hair had succumbed to the whispers of the afternoon's breeze. Samantha studied the figure, familiar, but so much younger than she felt. Actually, she looked considerably younger than her 47 years. She was athletic, and well proportioned and though her glasses concealed her eyes at the moment, they would reveal decades of attention, from her efforts to avoid the sun and her revered plastic surgeon. She made no apologies for the *"maintenance"* she had subscribed to in recent years. *Damn,* she thought, *you still got it girl!* But still, as she stared, she acknowledged how deceiving looks could be. Outward appearances provide no insight to the inner struggle. Surreal. She vaguely remembered the girl she was watching in the glass. Free spirit, happy, full of hope, ready to take on the world. Might she still be — Samantha removed her glasses, stepped up to the window — that girl? Not likely and she held back the tears working their way to the surface. A multitude of questions began to flood her thoughts. *Where are you Samantha? Where have you gone?* She reached out, touching her palm to its reflection, imagining herself splitting into two pieces. One happily residing in the present, one stubbornly planted in the past, her heart stuck somewhere in the middle. Palm to palm with her younger self, still touching the glass, trying to hold on to the memory of her. *Where have you gone . . . Enough,* she scolded herself as she turned to head back.

Samantha looked up at the lone cloud hovering above, floating along the canal with her, as she wandered along toward the Gritti. One of the city's charms was its lack of continuity, none of it made much sense to Samantha, but it didn't need to. It was, in large part, from the engineering of the numerous waterways, as much as from the need for its survival. Venezia's name had many derivations. She especially liked *"City of Masks"*. She'd decided that on her first visit. It had suffered, struggled and survived, as she had. The fact that the city was born out of fear, only to become one of the most treasured places in the world gave Samantha hope. Anyone could survive anything, if they put their mind to it. It was this orientation that earned her the *"Pollyanna"* nickname that followed her through college. Rose-colored glasses be damned, she didn't see herself as that. She was, if anything, too pragmatic at times. But she refused to believe that she was given this life, enduring the loss and pain she had, simply to exist as a miserable victim. She always chose to find a silver lining, even when it may very well be a strand of silver rope ready to hang her. She'd find reason to believe there was a bigger message, a better plan for her. And when she met Michael, she was quite certain it was fate placing her hand in his. But she did covet her masks, using them to shield the outside world from who she really was. A frightened young girl, with absolutely no idea how she'd make it through a day, much less a lifetime. Samantha continued to wander the streets of the old city aimlessly, no beginning, no end, no in-between. Buildings upon buildings lined the waterways, some with doors well below the water line, no longer functional. The hollow skeletons stared back at her, their very foundation under attack from nature's forceful hand for centuries. She couldn't help but smile at the comparisons she could make between her life and this city. The very lagoon that once offered Venice refuge was now the greatest threat to its survival. As did Michael, she concluded. The dreams they'd built their life on were now under attack and she was at a loss for how to save it, or even if she wanted to save it. *STOP*, she shouted to herself, recalling the exercise her therapist had given her to help her through her incessant overthinking, "Just tell the dialogue to stop and redirect your thoughts." She dug through her purse for her phone, and paused to call Kelly, thinking it odd she hadn't heard from her today, even given the time difference, Kelly had been adamant that they speak this morning. Straight to voicemail. Sam texted her:

"*WTH? Where are you sister, we need to talk. Call me, I'm alone for about an hour.*"

With that, she picked up her pace and the warm afternoon breeze from the canal provided a welcome cleansing effect on her. Samantha followed the cloud, overhead, as it danced with the sun to maintain centerstage. She had been so focused on the myriad of issues she was juggling that she'd lost track of her whereabouts. How fitting, she considered, just as Allegra so often urged her to do. She walked and walked, putting forth every possible scenario facing her right now. *Oh Michael, which way from here?* Her head shook back and forth as she replayed his midnight revelation. *Why you gotta do what you do?* She laughed out loud, *Today could be different — so different, if you'd just let me talk first. You could've skipped your soul-cleansing altogether. I could have told you we needed a break, I wanted it.* And there it was, the elephant in her room, she'd wanted it until *"it"* was no longer her choice. The very fact that he'd carried on a relationship over so many months led her to believe there was much more to the story than he'd shared. She understood, more than most because of what she kept in her head, words she refused to give life to, that asking and getting the full story would mean significant repercussions, the likes of which they may not recover from. So, at least for now, she decided, clasping her hands in a victorious air punch, she would leave that door closed. Leave those questions unanswered. *Damn you Kelly, why'd I listen, why'd I wait. Fuck . . .* She stomped one foot in front of the other, ready to race back to the hotel. Only when she gazed up to re-orient herself did she realize she was just around the corner. *Bless you Allegra, I walked, got lost and can almost feel my heartbeat again.*

Smiling to herself, Samantha entered the bustling lobby. The echoing noise briefly drowned out her persistent, relentless internal chatter. Patiently she waited for the elevator, noting she still hadn't heard from Kelly. *Hmmm. That girl,* she shook her head in frustration, *so damned undependable sometimes . . .* Michael sat stiffly on the sofa, scotch rocks in hand, when Samantha returned to the suite, quite a bit later than the hour she'd planned.

"Sorry, time got away from me. Won't take me but a minute to get ready."

"It's fine," he said coldly, as he sipped his drink. "I was worried though, you might have returned my call."

"What?"

She answered as she searched for her phone, to see his four missed calls and two from Kelly.

"Fuck, sorry, the ringer was off."

Fuck indeed, no wonder she hadn't heard from Kelly, and now their talk would have to wait until tomorrow when she returned to Florence.

"Take your time, I'm not going anywhere." He snarled as he poured another scotch and walked out to the balcony. Samantha watched him settle against the rail, leaning into the wind as it carried his hair from side to side. *Ooh, you sexy boy . . .* She smiled to herself and left him to his thoughts. Appearing just minutes later, Samantha was radiant, naturally so, wearing a simple black Prada sheath, black sandals, and the Asscher cut diamond studs Michael had given her when Ashley was born. Joining him on the balcony with her own cocktail, they soaked in the remaining minutes of sunlight together. Michael turned to her, pulling a box from his pocket. She recognized the packaging all too well, Bulgari. For as much as she didn't crave jewelry, this was her weak spot. Michael's first gift to her, a simple gold bracelet, was a treasure she wore to this day.

"What is this, Michael?"

She was suspicious of the timing, as well as the content, afraid to open it. Had he bought this for her, knowing what he'd be confessing last night? Was it even for her? Had he bought it for *"her"* and decided to give it to Samantha instead?

"Open it baby. I never made it to the gym. Dante called, he had a piece that had your name on it. He was right, I think. Open it!"

Slowly, Sam did just that. Right he was, the rose gold necklace took her breath away. Emerald upon emerald, eclipsed only by the perfectly cut diamonds. She knew the collection well, Giardini Italian, absolutely the perfect choice for her. Michael was thoughtful in that way. Without fail his gifts represented feelings, events, milestones and memories. Samantha appreciated the time he'd put into the act of giving. She knew he'd expressly chosen this necklace, acknowledging her passion for the Italian countryside, hoping to move her with this gesture and he'd succeeded. But still, there were his motives. She couldn't help but question them.

"Michael, come on. This? Now? I'm somewhat circumspect of your intentions, you have to know that."

"I do, Sam, believe me. But when I saw this, I had to get it for you. Please wear it tonight, just accept it, unconditionally, please."

"Ha ha . . . Oh I will, happily, you know how I love this line. Just don't for one fucking minute think it gets you off the hook you've hung yourself on." There was a lightness to her response, it surprised even her. How could she feel anything for him right now? But she did, oddly enough she mused, she felt easy, for the first time in what seemed like decades, she just let go. She saw a piece of herself, in that moment, the girl in the window. *Down the rabbit hole,* she thought, *I'm either falling deeper down it or crawling my way out of it. Either way, I suppose, it's good.* She smiled at Michael.

"I knew who I was this morning, but I've changed a few times since then." Now he believed, more than ever they had a chance. Samantha's quoting Lewis Carroll just then gave him a glimpse into her head that she'd never offer directly. Alice was one of her favorite characters. Michael often tried to gain a deeper understanding of her life, her past, but she let very few go there, down the rabbit hole, she'd say, was nowhere for the faint of heart to venture. And she'd slickly avoid divulging any substantive answer to his questions. He knew she'd suffered unimaginable loss during her childhood, from the bits and pieces she'd shared. Still, after all these years, he believed he was no closer to fully knowing his wife than he'd been that first night at the Uffizi. It frustrated him and at times angered him terribly. But Samantha had skillfully constructed her walls and not even he could penetrate them. Eventually he stopped trying, just accepting what she gave when she gave it. He was never completely sure she'd ever trust him enough to let him in. He hated to think that he had played a role in the demise of their relationship, but he knew damn well he had. He'd grown tired and impatient, constantly trying to get to her, understand her, get her to fucking talk. That was usually the way the arguments ended, "Will you just fucking talk to me?" He'd yell, then she'd yell back at him that he just didn't listen, so what would be the point, then storm out of whatever room they were in. Shutting it down, shutting him down. It was complicated, he conceded, their inherent approach to communication differed on almost every level. In the beginning those contradictions were intriguing, but as time dimmed love's sparkle, the differences had become irritations for both of them. For Samantha, the frustration was far more profound. Her history of communication wasn't working for her anymore, yet she couldn't work herself out of it. They'd found comfort in the disconnected repetitions of life. She couldn't quite admit that they'd come to take each other for granted. But somewhere between *"I do"* and *"I met someone,"* they'd lost sight of each other. Secrets had replaced memories. Just as she was about to broach the idea, the concierge called to let them know the car Allegra had sent was waiting. *Well,* she thought, *the dissection of our marriage can wait. So many decisions can wait. The next step can wait. Life can wait — for now.*

Allegra's home was warm and inviting, in-spite of what Michael considered the missing links of love and family. Gianni escorted them to the veranda. He'd been there by Allegra's side as long as Samantha had known her. An employee, make no mistake, but so much more. A trusted friend, almost family. She adored him. As far as Michael could tell, he'd been wrong, it would indeed be just the three of them tonight. This was unsettling, had Samantha already spoken to her? Was he about to be ambushed by the "Miu Miu Mafiati" as he often referred to the two of them? *Shit, this could completely suck,* he thought. Suddenly feeling sorry for himself and immensely insecure, he tucked his hand into hers as they approached Allegra, a show of solidarity and reassurance, he hoped.

"Bella, you are beautiful tonight. I'm so happy to see you."

She kissed Samantha, before taking a measured step back, "What's wrong my sweet girl?"

Allegra was nothing if not acutely attuned to Samantha's energy.

"I'm fine, mama, tired though and so hungry," Samantha giggled, brushing off her query.

"Of course darling, we'll chat later, when *he's* off on his way."

She wrapped her arm around Samantha's shoulder, leading her in from the veranda, while waving her hand at Michael, like a fly, a nuisance in the way of her getting to the bottom of whatever was gnawing at Samantha. Michael genuinely liked Allegra, but he always felt slightly insignificant around the two of them and she did little to assuage his anxiety. *You can't dismiss me lady, I'm here, I've been here for "your Sam" for 25 years, you can't say the same.*

"Allegra," Michael stood up to her, in a manner of speaking. "Where is everyone? This can't possibly be it for the night. Just us?" Samantha whipped around and shot him a look he knew he'd pay for later.

"Michael, I told you it would just be us, what's your problem?" She was fuming.

"Oh sweetheart, don't fault him, after all, it is a rare occasion that I prefer quiet company. Subdued," she smiled, "not generally a description equated with my personality." She let out a boisterous laugh. Forced, Samantha questioned, something was frightfully off about all of this. Especially her rush to defend Michael. Gianni escorted them in to dinner, table set to perfection, as always, with the exception of the seating. Allegra at the head, Michael directly to her left and Sam to his left. Oddly strategic, Michael presumed. The meal proceeded in starkly uneventful fashion, Allegra conspicuously demure and preoccupied. Even Michael was curious. Finally, she took a spoon to her wine glass, addressing the crowd of two, as if standing alone on the balcony, above the masses.

"Well, it seems my number has been delivered in rather undistinguished manner. We all have one, you know, just not the privilege of knowing its precise arrival time."

Michael took Samantha's hand onto his lap under the table as he saw the color slowly drain from her face.

"My doctors have informed me that I have ALS. No real prognosis, as far as how long I have left on this spinning ball of ours, not much they can do for me. Can you imagine that? All the money in this world I have and not a penny will spare my life."

Samantha had taken a sip of wine just as Allegra made her announcement. Her teeth clamped together, grinding away at the news, she couldn't swallow, fearful that any movement she made would unleash the tears welling up within her. The wine swished back and forth from the rocking motion of her clenched jaws, finally sliding down her throat into her knotted stomach. She was shaking, fighting her emotions as she twisted Michael's fingers through hers, squeezing ever tighter with each turn.

"You do see the irony here, I hope. Samantha, my angel, ALS, named after your famous American baseball player Lou Gehrig, wasn't it? You remember, I loved one of my own for years, can't remember his name, but those blue eyes matched his uniform, sheer splendor he was. I never had a chance. Could have married him, I think." She smiled, lost in her memories. She did know his name, she remembered all of the names, the places, the loves, but those were her stories to take with her. She had no intention of ever sharing all the layers of her life with others, they were hers and hers alone. Let others entertain themselves with conjecture, they'll do it anyway she rationalized. Even Samantha, whom she considered her daughter, was not privy to all there was to tell. Seeing Samantha struggle now, across the massive table, broke her heart. She knew how deeply this would hurt her little girl. How lost she'd been when they'd met, how she'd watched her grow up, become a wife, the most incredible mother and now a friend. A friend she'd have to say goodbye to far sooner than she'd ever hoped. But she couldn't postpone this, she had to tell her quickly. She really didn't expect to be with Samantha much longer and she wanted to prepare her. Prepare her as well as anyone can prepare those they will leave behind to carry on in their physical absence. Allegra's deep breath was startling, she coughed and stood.

"My loves, I'm tired. I know this is so much to process, let's get to rest. Bella, we will talk tomorrow. Michael," Allegra addressed him as though Samantha wasn't in the room. "I will depend on you here, you have strength and love, Samantha will need you now, as never before. Do not betray my love for you both." She lowered her head and looked up at him in a particularly admonishing fashion — the teacher to the pupil. He nodded in complete acquiescence. He could swear she knew what he'd done. He also knew that she'd never let it pass unanswered, even under these circumstances. Samantha had checked out. Her mind was reeling, along with her efforts to remain strong and she knew words were out of the question. She hugged Allegra as they parted for the night. The mammoth door clanked and shuttered in closing. A metaphor if ever she'd heard one. Gianni stood by the car, ready to drive them to the Gritti. Samantha and Michael answered him in concert, "We'll walk." She kissed Gianni's cheek and Michael extended a hand of thanks as they turned to leave.

It was still relatively early, so they headed toward the music and voices coming from St. Mark's Square, arms linked, holding each other up. The Venetian sky was lit up as the moon reached her fullness. A light, Samantha thought, a sign maybe. What that sign might be, she couldn't say. Michael, marriage, life, death, love. She opted to stop on love, the common fiber through it all, weaving its intricacies to and fro, creating the tapestry of her life. She'd like to wrap herself in that tapestry and roll it into the canal tonight. Float away to somewhere safe, happy, anywhere but here. Michael's arm tightened, she was slipping, in so many ways. He quickly lifted her into his arms, hugging her, an endearing reprieve. Her petite body faded into him, trembling, sobbing uncontrollably. *What sadistic wit the universe has,* she cursed inwardly, *this has been the worst 24 hours of my life. What next?* Her head tilted upward, pleading with the heavens. She regained her composure, and took Michel's hand. They walked forever, it seemed.

"Gelato?" Michael asked.

"Perfetto!" The way to her heart, always, she smiled. They sat, relaxed as they could possibly be, ordering espresso and gelato. The Piazza was alive tonight. Music, people, chatter, and the two of them. A couple, broken, lost, sadly unsure of where the next hours would take them.

"Let It Be, Michael, Let It Be." Her song for the moment, *Whisper words of wisdom. PLEASE!* She begged herself, nodding silently to the waiter as he set down their espressos.

"Did you even think of me when you were with "*her.*" She asked, not looking at him, as she lifted the drink to her lips. Michael hesitated, "Yes, of course." She knew it was a lie. She could see it in his eyes. She didn't blame him really. Why would he think of her? Why would he give thought to what he'd hoped to leave behind? It was a senseless question.

"Stupid, really, the question I mean. Don't bullshit me Michael, not now. Of course you didn't think of me, of us, of the consequences. If you did, you didn't care. Believe it or not, I get that. More than you'll ever know."

"What does that mean?" Michael suddenly realized that there was more to Samantha's current mood than she'd expressed.

"You're not the only one who's ever been unhappy, Michael. You didn't write the original score here." She stopped short of admitting her own secrets, the agenda she'd landed with. There would be time, the right time to open that box. For now, she'd let the music and energy in the Piazza take her away.

"**Grieving** death is easy.

It's tangible. How do we grieve **life**,

when it becomes something so different

than we'd ever imagined?"

Venice, Italy

SUNDAY, MARCH 12, 2017

Samantha threw herself onto the couch, as Michael opened the doors to the balcony and poured her a Prosecco. He kissed her lightly on the back of her neck and let her be. He appreciated the gravity of Allegra's news and that Samantha needed some time to try and make sense of it all. Of course, there were also her comments at the cafe in the Square. But he'd learned over the years that as pure as his intentions were in wanting to help her work through things, they generally backfired. She was a beautiful montage of emotional chaos. He loved her anyway, in spite of it — more likely because of it. It was her charm and her undoing, they'd both agree on that. And tonight, he'd honor that role, give her the space she craved and let her suffer alone. He watched her, adoringly, sadly, as he slipped past her into the bedroom, closing the door behind him.

Sipping mindlessly, letting the tears come, Samantha watched the clouds crisscross paths with the moon, in and out of darkness. Tonight's moon was full, as full as she could ever remember it. Its shadows painted broad, resplendent strokes across the sky. Black pearls, she thought — the varied hues of grey, blue and black, highlighted by creamy white sparkles, merging into one magnificent mirage across the Venetian horizon. La Bella Luna. Its movement was languid, like the ebb and flow of life itself, unpredictable and unforgiving. Allegra's announcement tonight was testimony to the harsh reality that life promises you no guarantees. Samantha waved her head back and forth, eyes wide open. *Now, then. Maybe, maybe not. Stay, go. It all seems so pointless, the planning, the hoping, the dreaming. What's the use?* She closed her eyes and drifted backwards in time . . . she felt as though she'd spent a large portion of her life waiting for the other shoe to drop. Tonight's news, just another in a long line of the *"what could have beens."* The thud of that dropping shoe always showed up when she was happiest. Teardrops turned into a fluid stream, down her cheeks, her neck, settling on her chest, melting into her heart. Each sip of Prosecco offered a momentary lapse from her pain. Each tear she shed brought forth a memory.

Four years old: No real memory of Dad, a boating accident had taken his life. What could I possibly remember? Only what I saw in pictures and heard over the years. A champion water-skier, ironically taken by the sea that filled his life with joy everyday.

Five years old: Kelly left me to be a star on Broadway. Yeah, that didn't fare so well, for either one of us.

Thirteen years old: Mom died. She never shared just how sick she was, until she said goodbye in my arms. She was so frail. A hollow shell of the woman she'd been and the woman I struggle to remember until I was ten. When life was good. And then it wasn't.

Seventeen years old: College, Italy, Michael, marriage, motherhood. My life as I'd dreamt it would be, most of it anyway. The early years, with the children, there was no shoe drop there. They were every bit of every dream I'd ever had. More so really, than I deserve. I look into their eyes and wonder what it would have been like. How it would feel to pick up a phone and call Mom, share milestones, victories, heartaches. I had to fumble about to start our own holidays and traditions, why couldn't she be here to teach me? Why did she leave me to figure out this whole fucking thing on my own? Some days it was all a beautiful dream, others a completely tragic mess. My mess that I have absolutely no idea how to clean up. "Keep going," she'd say, "it's all we can ever do." Well I don't know how to do that now. Michael in the arms of another woman, in her bed, in her heart. Now Allegra, at least I can be there for her. God bless her for having the courage to tell me now. Please give me the strength to be who she needs me to be. And Michael . . . Michael . . . I can't imagine doing this without him. When my shrink asked me to consider who I'd want by my side if I were terminally ill or worse — I couldn't answer her. Even having just gone through my treatments, I couldn't answer her. I didn't want to answer her. Now I know, maybe I've always known, Michael. Always Michael . . .

Ironic you know. Everyone of you lost, suffered, left me — in spite of a deck that seemed stacked in your favor. Really, Dad? A champion skier and you die on a boat? Mom, you never ventured outside of the box or over the lines. You lived a kind, healthy life, and you succumb to the ugly, disfiguring demise of cancer? Allegra, you contract the one disease that encapsulates your mind, keeping it alive while destroying your body? How cruel is that, your lively laughter, your sweet voice will be silenced till the end and you'll have to spend every waking hour observing, living, unable to respond. Michael, you were so miserable with us that you decided another woman would make you that much happier? I wasn't a good enough wife, lover? You had to see what you were missing? See if maybe it could get any better?

Jesus, no matter how you play it, the cards shuffle themselves and leave you holding a hand you didn't plan for. We think we are making the choices, writing our stories, it's all bullshit. Nothing in this world is by our design. We're just stuck with outcomes we didn't prepare for, circumstances out of our control and hopefully the strength to pick up the pieces and keep going. There you go mama . . . 'Just keep going . . . '

Samantha opened her eyes, she'd followed her memories into a deep sleep. As she regained focus, she noticed Michael on the balcony, his robe billowing in the wind, the constant thrum of the water traffic on the canal climbing up the columns drowned out her internal dialogue. A sight, surprisingly, given her current mood, that turned her on. She tiptoed up behind him, aching to get a sense of where his heart was at that instant. Wrapping her arms around his waist, she noticed he was intently watching something across the canal.

"What are you doing? What time is it?"

"Shhhh . . . . Look, there . . . the third floor window. Watch."

As she looked outward, the angel perched atop the Basilica di Santa Maria della Salute, across the waters caught her eye. Spinning with each gust of wind, as if searching for a direction to settle on. The church, built in the 1600's to honor Mary for delivering Venice from the Plague, was a fitting backdrop for their marriage. Samantha, adrift in her own debris, was looking for an answer, some sort of sign. *Ha,* she thought, *of course this is my sign.* She turned to follow Michael's finger across the water, into the room on the third floor, voyeuristically taking in the view that had Michael so entranced. Across the canal, under the spotlight of the full moon, Samantha and Michael watched three lovers passionately engulfed in a wild expression of love or lust. Whatever it was, they couldn't tear themselves away. Two women, and one man, she laughed to herself at that, knowing full well it was Michael's ultimate fantasy, every man's she suspected.

"Oh my God," she whispered, smiling, eyes as big as the moon overhead.

"I can't stop watching . . . " He was adolescent in his excitement.

"How long have they been at it?" Wondering at the same time, how long he'd been glued to the exhibition.

"An hour? I don't know, I came out about one." he shrugged a guess, having lost all track of time.

"Ha! You're a sick fuck! It's three-thirty!"

She strained to keep her laughter quiet as she turned

her back to him, pulling his arms around her shoulders, interlocking fingers, shimmying her ass up to him. He was hard, full, just the way she liked it. The girls danced over the man, laying him down on the bed. Samantha, added her own soundtrack to the scene, Marvin Gaye's, "Sexual Healing."

"Get up . . . Get up . . . Get up . . . Get up . . . "

Swaying as she whispered the words to Michael, grinding further in to him with each word. She was awed by what she was watching. Raw sensuality, a live performance and they had a private audience. The girls kissed while atop their male partner, cupping each other's breasts as he lay under them, a prisoner of sorts. Eroticism, fantasy, escape, she couldn't be happier.

Then, slowly she turned, giving all of her attention to Michael. She stood, perfectly still, as he unzipped her dress and let it fall to her feet. Leaving her black lace Cosabella panties and bra in place, he let out a deep sigh. Mouth, cock, hands, lips, breasts, a seductive symphony unfolding, until she couldn't take any more. Wet, hot, craving him as she once had, Samantha leaned in to Michael, placed his hands on each of her breasts, planting her lips on his, sucking in his wanting tongue. Michael followed her lead, taking over instantly. He flipped her around, allowing his back to rest on the balcony ledge, not a care in the world for who might be watching them. Dropping to his knees, he slid his head between her legs, fingers and tongue followed, pushing aside her panties. She squealed, sliding her torso against his lips. She honestly couldn't recall the last time he'd taken her like this. Nor could she remember wanting it as she did tonight. His head pulsating, in and out with every charge of his tongue, partaking in the joy of every ounce of her sweet, salty pussy. She writhed, unable to remain still, sliding to her knees, pulling his head up to kiss him. Their lips locked, arms entangled, hearts longing — searching for some spark of magic that had been lost. Tonight, on the balcony of the Donghia Patron Grand Canal Suite, in the Gritti Palace, in Venice, Italy, they found it.

They'd never stayed in this particular suite. Allegra had booked it. The decor was a perfectly executed display of the contemporary, minimalist work of American designer Angelo Donghia. Such a drastic departure from the traditional Italian antiques and lavish interiors of most of the suites. Then there was the record player and vinyls from the seventies. Better than Disneyland, she'd mentioned to Michael as they'd settled in earlier. How fun it was for her to have all this musical history at her fingertips. Samantha couldn't help smiling, watching the night progress as it did. She imagined Allegra had personally orchestrated the intoxicating, sensual sonata before them. Maybe it was the setting or that Allegra knew the trio across the canal and hoped to provide an escape, or that she'd just tried to give the two of them a reprieve from the devastating news she'd planned to share. She couldn't have known the far-reaching impact of her choices. The art, the music, the couch situated to view the Canal, and tonight, the sex-capades of the strangers across the turbulent waters. *Oh Allegra,* Sam thought, *you did well. You did really, really well.*

The moon's glimmer casting its spell, they were oblivious to the world around them, and to the fact that they were exposed there on the balcony, for all to see. Not a care in the world, this was their time, fleeting as it may be. Both were completely naked, in every sense of the word. They were only beginning to peel back the layers, wounds years in the making. Ripping off life's band aids — work, children, school, activities, vacations, holidays — the *"everything"* that overshadows love's beginnings. How deep those wounds were remained to be seen, talked through, shared. Could they be healed, could their life together be saved?

Life, Samantha surmised, *does whatever it wants, in spite of your plans, instead of them. The proverbial snowball of life gains momentum as it rolls down the mountain and your only hope for survival is to jump on for the ride. You have no clue where it will take you and what it will leave you with in the end. And what a crazy fucking ride this has been . . .*

She threw her head back in wild abandon, wrapping her legs around him. He slid his hands under her ass, lifting her just enough to sit atop his thighs. They rocked, each to their own melody, bodies sweating, hearts pounding. Sam wriggled further on top of him, sliding his hard cock into her. Deeply into her, she wrapped both arms around his neck and buried her head, buried her heart, buried her past, their past.

"Let It Be," she whispered, "just Let It Be."

Samantha was different tonight, he noticed. He hadn't expected this response, but he loved it, every fucking part of it, he'd missed this girl. Without pause, he lifted her, flipped her over onto her knees, on the marble ground and took her from behind, holding her hair with one hand, her breasts with the other. Tonight was an unrefined and passionate encounter. Samantha responded in kind, slipping out of his grasp, she stood and began moving to the music in her head. She danced in front of him until he couldn't take any more. Michael stood, clasped her hands in his, wrapped them around his waist and carried her inside. Gently now, he laid her across the living room floor. Spread eagle she welcomed him in, wrapping her long, tanned legs around his neck, pulling him ever deeper in to her. Together they moved in harmony with the sounds from the canal. Clank, clank, clank, the gondolas tied below feuding with the cresting waters. Crashing into the docks, then sloshing back with the receding current. Their pace followed, slowly at first, increasing with the tide's rolls, heated from their desire until they both exploded into each other. Michael dropped onto her, breathless, and spent. Unanticipated feelings surging, this had been the woman of his dreams, once, so long ago, and here she was again, tonight, with him. He prayed it was a beginning, not an ending. He prayed she'd forgive him. She rested her head on his shoulder, his head buried in her chest.

"I love you, baby, I love you," Michael whispered, kissing her neck, his heartbeat slowing down, calm replacing the storm within him. Samantha breathed the salty winds off the canal as they gently knocked the veranda doors about.

"Michael — I keep asking myself, where did we go? How did we lose this?"

"I know. I mean, I don't know the answer" he chuckled, remembering that his normal response would drive her crazy.

"I know what you mean. But thank you for that, for remembering."

"Sammie, I don't know where to start, I fucked this up. I . . ."

"Stop! You did fuck this up."

She gently swept his hair back on his forehead.

"I have so many questions, I just don't want the answers tonight."

She rolled off of him onto her back, laying her head back down on his chest, speaking into him. "I can't decide how much I really want to know, to be honest. I always believed I'd take it to my grave if it were me. If I did what you say you've done. So you're gonna have to wait, but when I ask, promise me you'll answer. Don't fucking bull-shit me — not now."

"I promise."

They both knew that was probably a lie. He'd likely tell her just enough to move on, just enough to spare hurting her anymore than he already had. Just enough to put her fears and insecurities to rest. There was no do-over here. He'd put it out there. His secret had now become their story and she had to find a way to live with it. Samantha closed her eyes, feeling exactly what Michael was think-ing, and thinking it for herself. She'd never divulge all of anything. Of course, part of that was just her nature, she kept so much inside. But the cold reality of it here and now was that she'd no more tell Michael everything she'd ever done than to jump off their balcony for a night swim in the canal. Infidelity was a personal choice. Samantha had always believed confessing to *"clear a conscience"* was a copout. Because then it became the partner's heartbreak to deal with as well. It was a secret, she believed, the person committing the act deserved to live with, to suffer, not their innocent partner. Trust. She wasn't sure that once it was lost, it could ever completely be found. She really did battle with both sides, hoping never to actually have to choose a course of action. Or, non-action. She shook off the thoughts and looked into Michael's eyes.

"This was impulsive, Michael," she grinned. "But isn't that what we all crave? Maybe? Maybe it's the familiarity of a life together that kills it in the end. Maybe it's being open to these kinds of spontaneous moments and just letting them happen that keeps love breathing."

Michael was listening, surprised at the depth of the conversation. He wasn't so sure she meant to have it with him. Aloud. "Sam, do you really believe that? Is our life dead to you?"

"Really, Michael?" she was annoyed, "you're the one who's been living a completely separate life for the past year, one fucking lie after another? Is that alive for you, is that a family? Am I missing something here? Do you honestly think that I believe for one minute that you just *"happened"* across this woman? Give me a break." She turned her back to him.

"No, I don't, and I don't expect you to understand it all. I don't fucking understand it all. That's why I asked you. The idea, that love could be dead, too familiar. When you put it like that, the answer is NO!" He was animated, sitting up, taking her shoulders in his hands. "What I'm asking is how we let it get to a point where we both thought that our life together wasn't worth protecting. And, no I don't blame you, I didn't protect it, I let someone else in. But Sam . . . it takes two people. Both of us — in or out. We were not protecting each other, loving each other."

He stopped, looked directly in to Samantha's eyes, and saw something in her, a deeply grounded confidence. She was offering clarity, strength, and insight to the situation. He was awed by her energy right now. Samantha had always leaned on him, looked to him to take care of her, the family, their life. He'd never questioned that role. In fact, he expected it — *"old school"* he'd told her over and over. But now, he was watching the very woman he'd vowed to care for till death they do part, taking care of him. Posing questions and seeking answers that may very well determine the future of their life together.

"Michael, I understand more than you think. I also understand that life is messy and love is complicated and we've been through a lot these past years. I'm not so sure it's dead, but our love is not well, we are not well or we wouldn't be here, having this conversation. I also know that tomorrow's another day, we have a lot to work through and even more decisions to make. And none of it is going to come easily or quickly. We keep talking . . . deal?"

"Deal, baby."

He laid back down, hugging her and they kissed. The long, slow, precious kisses of their past. *"Blame it on the kisses,"* Michael used to say, telling her that he was lost to her forever when they kissed — that their lips were perfectly matched.

She'd ruminate on this stream of thought, she knew that, but for tonight, for now, she could actually buy into the concept of one love. A lifetime, a partnership that, even with its tumult, could survive, thrive even and be exciting. She could believe that tonight. She needed to believe that tonight. She needed all of that, whether it held up in the morning light or not. It was real, tangible and believable tonight as she lay in his arms. The arms she'd once wanted wrapped around her until her last breath. *Enough,* she thought, *I need sleep.* Michael had fallen into it, breathing lightly as he lay on her chest. She watched him, wondering if it was her name wandering through his dreams. Or the woman he claimed he'd left behind, his *"mistake"*. *Where have your dreams taken you Michael?* She lifted herself to see him in the shadow of the moon's light. There would have to be more, she'd have to ask the questions consuming her subconscious, but right now, she would sleep. She could tuck the past 24 hours away, go back to the night in Florence in their suite at the St. Regis. The arms of a man who would change everything. Her detour. She hadn't thought of that term in ages. Calling him that once during their early days, explaining to him that she'd had a plan for her life and then she'd met him and the plan no longer mattered. She'd opted to take the detour, reckless as it seemed. Maybe, just maybe, she needed to revisit the concept. These past five years, the children beginning to leave, his affair, her starring role in bad decision theater, all a detour leading them here. Back to each other. Could that possibly be? Her eyes grew heavier until she surrendered to her exhaustion, sliding into sleep. She welcomed the chance to escape, to dream, to give her gypsy soul a rest.

"What do you do with the **fantasy?**

When reality **isn't** at all what

you envisioned."

Venice, Italy

SUNDAY, MARCH 12, 2017

The morning sun woke them, still on the floor, entwined in each other's arms, the wind blowing thru the doors they'd left open last night. The room was as they'd left it, but nothing about them was the same. Michael kissed her before jumping up to shower. As raw and ridiculously physical as the night had become, it was somewhat of a turning point. Samantha was deeply touched, she loved Michael. Was it possible that in the midst of their complete disregard for each other, they could find their way back? She had no reservations in admitting this to herself. Conceding to the realization that, given an alternative existence, she just might opt to stay, to tend to this garden she'd planted so many years before. She'd once read that *"the grass is always greener where you water it."* Hadn't given it much thought until just now as she watched him move about the room packing, muttering to himself. *It's true,* she thought, *we all crave attention and where we decide to give it, from whom we take it, this is where we thrive.* This was a lot for her to take in, given the man that she was watching now, the one who'd allowed another to water his plants, blindsided her, shook her foundation to its core with his soul-baring. She still couldn't wrap her head around the why and the timing. But the reality of it all wasn't really so complicated. She could leave, look for a new love, build a new life. Or, she could stay and try to get past all of it. And not just his betrayal, but hers. She may not have shared her thoughts yet, but they were very real and a critical part of her consideration now. She wouldn't decide, definitely wouldn't discuss any of it with him, just yet, but the wheels were turning.

When you just think of leaving, it's easy, the idea of it all, the fresh start. A chance to right all the wrongs of the past. But then there it is, the open door, right in front of you and . . . what the hell do you do? Samantha contemplated the choices that lay in front of her. Both sides, the consequences and collateral damage of choosing either of the options she had. Mentally, she began to view the landscape of each:

Leave: I've got good reason now. He cheated, he lied, he lived a lie for the better part of a year. He brought this on himself, so he should suffer the consequences. How different will my life become? What will it look like? Splitting up all we've built together, the family, the businesses, the home, the memories. The memories yet to come — weddings, births, holidays. Who really suffers, who stands to lose the most? Michael? Me? The children, they didn't ask for this. How do they fare? Do they choose sides, separate from each other and from us, to sift through the wreckage of a life they never anticipated? Do they hate us, one

of us more than the other, for disrupting their utopia and tearing their family apart? I can't let every possible reaction of our grown children dictate my decision, cloud my judgment. They're off living their own adult lives. They'll have to come to terms with whatever course of action Michael and I pursue. They will come around, they want us to be happy — right? They want us to live out our lives in joy, if not with each other, at least with the possibility of being happy again, they have to want that for us, for me.

Stay: This seems to be the simplest choice. Keep it all together. Keep us all together. We have to find a new and better way to be a couple. Just the two of us — and the dogs! It means letting go of a lot of anger and insecurities. It would be so much better for the children. Adult lives aside, they are our children and they deserve to have their family together. It's the only family they've ever known. That does mean something to me. It's also about not giving up. I've never "left". I don't do that. I keep trying, whatever it takes. I keep working to make a situation better. Maybe staying is not the simpler choice — but rather the stronger choice. Maybe it's the one outcome I can control. By not giving up, by giving all of this another chance, just maybe the story I write can have a happy ending. Stay . . . just stay . . .

Samantha stopped, realizing that a great deal of her fear, was rooted in the dismantling of her family and how it would affect her. Would they hate her for leaving? Acknowledging the *"unintended consequences"* of every move she made now, the severity and perhaps irreparable damage that she might do. Not just to their immediate existence, but the long term impact — their future personal relationships, their relationships with each other and, of course, their relationships with her and Michael. Samantha knew this was no longer just her decision. Regardless of what got them there, whose bad behavior was worse, this belonged to both of them to work through for better or worse — together. Just as they had started this grand experiment — no road map but with big dreams and love for each other. Could those dreams and that love carry them through what lay ahead?

Michael walked over to her, showered, refreshed. "Get ready, we're going out. I'll finish packing us, the concierge will take our bags."

Samantha smiled at his assertiveness, she appreciated him taking the lead, unsure where he was taking her but okay with that right now. She'd had enough introspection and *"life-figuring"* for the time being. She hopped to her feet, reached up, and kissed him.

Sunday mornings throughout the old city were quiet, the tourists sleeping in, the residents in prayer. There was a sereneness to it all. The Gritti's private Riva speedboat was waiting for them at the dock. The waters had calmed from the night's tides, the warming sun was just bright enough to host their ride pleasantly.

"I can't remember the last time we did this! Michael, it's fabulous."

Samantha snuggled into his arms, leaning back to soak up the rays and the salt air.

"Sam, look." Her eyes followed his hand pointing to the

column, the Lion of Venice, perched high above the west entrance to the Piazza San Marco, the Patron Saint's symbol, found in various forms throughout the city. Most often, the Lion is shown with its paw laid upon an open book:

'Pax tibi, Marce, Evangelista meus'

"Peace be with you," she whispered to Michael. It was a sign, she believed that with all her heart. Legend says that the angel that visited St. Mark said those words to him, that Venice would be his final resting place. "You know this is it for us. A final resting place for *this*." She rolled her hands wildly about their faces, extending her arms toward the sky, referring to their state of affairs.

"You and your signs," he chided, but this time he saw it too. "Sammie, we're not done, I believe this with every fiber in my body."

"I know," she replied, "I feel it too. I'm not ready for the end, although I did picture kicking your ass into the canal as we boarded, but so many witnesses, the mess, the explaining . . . "

She laughed, she joked, and Michael breathed the fresh air of relief. He inhaled deeply the potential of hope for them both.

"Ha! I'd have dragged you in with me, girl." He kissed the top of her head and wrapped his arms tightly around her. This was indeed a sign — a chance to begin again. The music from the piazza fell quiet as they encircled the lagoon. Michael directed the captain to drop them off at Piazza San Marco. He wanted to walk with her, see the city as she loved it, on foot, detour upon detour upon detour. And so they walked, lost in the city for *"getting lost and being found,"* as Allegra fancied to describe it. Ducking under bridges, kissing, giggling, whispering to each other like teenagers.

There's an easiness to fall into — regardless of the tortured path you walk together. She considered their years together, the familiarity that comes from creating a family and spending so much time with each other.

"There is something new to be found in something old, Michael. A re-birth of sorts. It's here for us now." She gazed upward to him as they approached the Gritti. "Let's just see where it all takes us."

"I'm there baby, I'm there . . . "

"Is marriage an accumulation of **broken dreams** and promises? How do you go on when you just can't take the weight of it all?"

Florence, Italy

SUNDAY, MARCH 12, 2017

Samantha relaxed on the train ride back to Florence, even if only a temporary reprieve. She watched Michael doze off, before turning to the window, gazing out as the train rolled across the Italian countryside. Spring had come to Tuscany. The fields were beginning to bloom now, offering new life as far as the eye could see — fiery hues of gold, red orange, and yellow radiant beneath the sinking sun. Each frame offered Samantha a different perspective, the calm of the rambling hills, farm houses sprinkled about, wildflowers waving in the breeze. She thought back to her first ride from Rome to Milan with her mother when she was eight. Mesmerized by today's views, they called up the memory as vividly as if it were yesterday, along with the countless trips to Venice to see Allegra. Her heart sank just then, pushing Allegra's dire news to the forefront. She'd successfully tucked it away these past hours, but with the tears rippling through her now, she had to strain to maintain her composure and re-focus on the landscape. The vastness, the history, the simplistic beauty of it all. Tuscany had lured her in early on, taking hold of her heart, never letting go — it was home. At thirteen, she and Kelly had strewn their mother's ashes across the valley just northwest of Florence, and come back to visit numerous times. Ultimately, she settled on her course of study in landscape architecture. Samantha felt a closeness to the land here that she'd never experienced before and even now she believed the direction of her life had led her back at exactly this moment in time to bring her clarity. All the paradoxes and choices she was facing, Tuscany understood, she understood — the answers would come.

Samantha dug through her carry-on and pulled out her journal, anxious to read her most recent entries. When she thought about her state of mind on the plane over, what she'd written, and then Michael's revelations this past weekend, she was clearly in conflict. Could she write it out of her? Could she find sense on the pages here? She nestled back into the comfort of her seat, tucking her feet up underneath her left hip and pressed her shoulder and head fully against the window. It reminded her of herself as an eight-year-old child seeing the magnificent countryside for the first time. She popped in her ear buds, slowly scrolling through the playlists, before settling on "Seventeen", an aptly named 80's collection of Stevie Nicks, Quarterflash, Billy Joel, Bonnie Raitt, Boz Scaggs, The Motels and Quincy Jones. It was Sam's mantra — *"On the Edge"*, her *"safe place"* she told Michael in their early days. She found comfort living on the edge, keeping him on the edge. Sam was solidly grounded in the 80s — musically, emotionally — stuck in 1981, specifically. That was the year her life changed forever — at 13.

Where was that girl, she questioned. *I'm tired of waiting. I'm not afraid. I'm ready for this life.* The realization that she really did see her future differently than she had even five months ago — two days ago for that matter, brought a huge smile to her face. Satisfaction. She dwelled upon that briefly as the sun disappeared behind the hilltops. *I'm okay — this will be okay. It doesn't get any worse than this weekend!* She shook off the consideration of such absurdity. *Oh my God, I can do any of this, deal with any of this — how I need to. I don't even feel the slightest bit nervous right now. I've got this. Ok empty-nester syndrome — whatever the hell you are — you are my bitch now!* Samantha laughed to herself imagining a standing ovation from the crowd of well-wishers who'd been by her side as she'd begun the slow descent into her post-full-time mom nightmare. For the first time in forever it seemed, she honestly believed she had answers and direction. But more than any of that, she felt she had the wherewithal to see it through. Michael, their marriage, Allegra, going home to an empty house and a city that no longer fit. The worst things that she could ever have imagined were happening. *Bring it on baby,* she told herself, *I. Am. Ready.* Her eyelids shut, she spun the volume up as loud as she could tolerate, losing herself in the music and the memories. Her journal lay closed on her lap.

"Babe," Michael whispered to her, nudging her shoulder, "Florence."

"Oh my gosh, that was quick!"

"You were in such a deep sleep, I hated to wake you."

Still drowsy, Samantha stiffened her back, working to regain composure as she shifted about in her seat — reaching for her journal — where was it? A sigh of relief, she saw that it had fallen to the floor. But panic quickly replaced her calm, had Michael read it while she slept? She studied his face and energy as nonchalantly as possible while she gathered her belongings. *No way,* she assured herself, *he wouldn't — he couldn't.* She looked up once more as she stood, searching his eyes. *Nope,* she felt confident that he'd not read any of it. Not that he couldn't, she rationalized, just that he shouldn't. It was hers, private and there were feelings she was not ready to share. *Fuck, I hope not.* She picked up her things and followed him down the platform to their waiting car and the ten-minute ride back to the Four Seasons. It wasn't late, but she was exhausted.

"Dinner in the room?" Michael asked, feeling equally tired and not interested in socializing.

"Yes, was just thinking that. It's been a long couple of days, I'm spent. Tonight — easy, early — please?!"

Michael draped his arm across her shoulder, falling a step behind as they made their way though the crowded lobby out the doors and across the grounds to the Garden Suite.

"I've got to meet Carlo in Sesto in the morning, I'll be up and out by eight."

"Okay." Samantha replied, a bit relieved, she welcomed the alone time. "You know I won't be bored," she gently elbowed his rib, "maybe a massage, I don't know, I'll see how I feel tomorrow. How long will you be?"

"Should be back by lunch. Let's plan on 1:30, you pick the place."

"Sure, sounds good." Samantha ducked behind him as he unlocked the door. Turns out he hadn't just read her mind, he'd anticipated her answer and the very cravings she'd had since leaving Venice. Fausto was waiting on the patio, a sumptuous meal spread out before them. She inhaled the flavors as they floated across the cool night air — grilled Steak Florentine, and freshly made pasta. She hadn't realized just how hungry she was.

"God, Michael, this is divine! Thank you."

He just smiled, one more thing he'd always adored — Sam loved to eat. She had no use for the women who lunched on lettuce. She enjoyed everything about eating — the talk, the smells, the texture — the feelings. She ate well and took care of herself, indulging as she pleased, knowing she'd found that balance, even if other scales in her life were completely out of whack.

The garden was aglow under the moonbeams. Not nearly as bright as last night in Venice, but light enough to thwart off the black sky and give full attention to the candle's flicker. This was paradise, Samantha thought, *even in the darkest hour, she shines through.* She was curiously obsessed with the moon. Its energy, its light, its watchful eyes. *Maybe,* she fathomed, *it's the pieces of everyone we've lost, taking care of us, looking out for us . . .* Samantha was a romantic, but really more of a spiritual soul, searching for life's meaning, the signs to let her know it wasn't all a ruse. That her life had meant more than its sheer physical presence. That the grand design had a greater purpose for her, for everyone. The ups, the downs, the good, the bad, there had to be more to it — if not in this life then somewhere — sometime. She'd followed this road, more so, over the past few years, studying various philosophies, practicing yoga, meditation, seeking spiritual guidance and understanding. It was not something she'd spent a lot of time discussing with Michael. He wasn't dismissive, but he didn't see the purpose for her quest. From his perspective she had it all. What could she possibly need or want that she didn't already have, that he hadn't provided in their life together? It then became an ego issue — he took her feelings personally as failure on his part and she grew angry at his making it all about him. They fought often and left it all unresolved, just getting back to the business of living. *"Band-aids,"* she'd tell him, "we never really rip the scabs off, the wounds never really heal. We just cover the surface and hope they disappear, repair the damage themselves. None of which ever happens." He'd get angrier, more frustrated and the cycle would begin again.

And so she headed down the self-discovery road alone, at least separate from him. How could he understand where she was, if she hadn't included him in her journey? While she questioned it at times, she also knew it was pointless, he wasn't there — physically or spiritually. He wasn't going through the same things. His life had no dramatic shift when Steven went to college. Her life turned upside down and she was trying to find her way back. Trying to find some way to move beyond the past 25 years when being a mother was the most important aspect of her life, the reason for her existence, as she saw it. She was at the same time, the happiest she could be, three children successfully on their way in life. Becoming the beautiful, strong individuals she'd prayed they'd be. They were all so close, so it wasn't abandonment she felt. It was an inexplicable emptiness, she had absolutely no idea what to do next, and she was heartbroken, lost, struggling to stay afloat in the life she'd been left with. She was better with a plan, ready for what was next — a purpose. But none of it made sense anymore. What the hell was she supposed to do now? Who would she become, who could she become? She'd spent the last quarter century raising children and being Michael's utility player. She'd worked herself out of the marketplace and had no idea what was next.

Then there was Dallas. Michael did know the depth of her disdain for the city. She'd never considered it home, just that place she ended up when she married him. She missed the west coast, the ocean and now that the kids were gone she voiced that more often than he could stand. He grew tired and impatient, listening to her complaints and musings of a better life in California. Resentment invariably led to more arguments, then to shutting each other out. Michael spending more and more time working and traveling and Samantha developing new friendships and interests. But she just couldn't stand wandering the halls of their massive, now empty home. It was too much, at least then it was. Hard to believe only two years earlier, after Steven left, she'd viewed her life so differently.

The door closed behind her as she leaned on it — staring at the stairs, the emptiness of the house brought her to her knees. Sobbing uncontrollably — months of preparation and building to this moment. Here, by herself, unsure of everything that lay before her. Steven was the last out the door to college, Michael was out of the country and she was here "holding it all together" as Michael had told her she needed to do now. To keep their life in Dallas going as he continued to build it around the world. Trouble was, she didn't want that now, the life here. She was lonely and lost and tired of following his lead. There had to be answers, soon, she was spiraling out of control and needed to catch herself before it was too late.

Samantha was glad to be alone, though it amplified the overwhelming sense of being alone. How could she be this sad? It wasn't a surprise, it was life, children grow up, you raise them to leave, to be good citizens in the world, independent souls. But, she wondered as she looked up, through her tears, across the stillness of the rooms around her, 'now what?' She was relieved that Michael was out of the country today, she didn't want to have to explain or excuse her feelings. She needed to figure them out first before his barrage of criticisms, questions and dismissing. He had that way about him when he didn't want to deal with something she was going through, whatever that was. Michael was not a micro-manager and he was intolerant of that role with Samantha. He expected her to take care of things and not bother him with the "petty bullshit" as he often reminded her. He wasn't particularly unique in that regard, she thought. Maybe it was a gender thing — women worry and obsess about things said and done so much more than any man would. Samantha was involved in the kids' schools and several charities, all carrying with them difficult social complexities and dynamics. She'd be the first to admit that she didn't always handle all the personalities involved in the best manner, burning more bridges than she'd built over the years. During those early days, she was an all-or-nothing girl, impulsive and stubborn. She gave everything she had to all that she did, but she never quite mastered the art of balancing the myriad of temperaments involved with the tasks at hand and the end game most often suffered. She often blamed her age, so much younger than Michael and ill-prepared for the life he'd thrust upon her. But that challenge was what drove her — to succeed and prove the naysayers wrong. She did have her moments and victories. But here today, she felt like the 22-year-old college girl he'd wooed in Florence and married three months later with no idea what the future would bring. The big difference now was she had the future, the life she'd dreamt of then and now it was gone. She was on her own again, in a manner of speaking. The canvas was blank — she held the brush in her hand with no clue of where to begin painting — or what for that matter. There it was . . .

Here she was — still — five years later. Did they have a life together without the kids? She'd begun wrestling with that during Robert's senior year. She and Michael were growing apart, not intentionally, it was just happening. Their interests had changed and their communication fell victim to those changes. Talking less, except for the essential dailies, and loving less. Maybe that was the key. Their physical relationship had always been active and fun, she knew it was special when she considered the lives of her friends, listening to them complain endlessly about their "missing" husbands and the choices they made to survive the loneliness. She didn't judge them, but she did think about what she'd do if she were that alone. Then the cancer diagnosis came. Anything wrong with the everyday was shelved, it just seemed to fade away. No resolutions, just back-burnered. Michael was there though, emotionally, physically supportive as he had not been recently, so it was easy to leave their disconnected relationship behind and focus on the challenges they faced together. Not life-threatening, but life-altering without question. Yet once the positive results continued to come in, life slowly fell back into step. What troubled them before returned with more weight and vengeance. Now time had eroded even their physical connection and she was once again alone. She was in a free-fall with no parachute, no closer to answers, no idea where to turn or who to turn to. For the first time since Michael kissed her in the moonlight on the banks of the Arno, Samantha felt completely on her own and unsure of her future.

And yet, this was the road . . . this was the time she knew she had to step up and decide how it should look from here on out. It was up to her to decide what she wanted her legacy to be. She had a lot to consider now — coming back to Italy to care for Allegra, her relationship with Michael in light of his infidelity, and professionally. She knew now that she did want to re-enter the work force, to pursue the work she'd left behind when they'd married. That excited her when she spent time with the idea and considered the possibilities. The landscape of all she'd studied had changed so dramatically over the years. It would take time and reflection to see where she fit in and what she wanted to accomplish. That prospect was the one certainty she had right now. She was ready to accept the challenges and re-establish her relevance in the world. She was finding her voice and she liked how it sounded, most importantly how it felt. These were her days in front of her now, and dammit, she would create the life she wanted this time. She would fill the blank pages.

"Michael," Samantha sipped her wine before continuing, "do you ever think about our beginning?"

"I do, all the time. Especially being here with you where it started. I knew the minute I saw you, spent that first night with you — it would be you — only you."

"Only me?"

Her jab was light, but meaningful. Only her until it wasn't only her.

"I thought that too, but then it all happened so fast. Think about it. We met and got married here three months later, before I would have returned home. Why did we rush it all?"

"It didn't feel rushed — it felt right. Period. At least it did to me."

"I know, I felt it too, then. But looking back — I wonder."

"Wonder what? If you loved me? Or if you made a mistake?"

"Both really. I loved you, I still love you."

He opened his mouth, raising his hand to speak.

"Stop it, Michael, let me finish. You always talk over me. Stop!"

"Fine, talk, tell me how the past 25 years were a mistake, how I haven't taken care of you, given you an amazing fucking life . . . "

"Are you serious? That's where you go here? Again?! It always finds its way back to being about you. Get the fuck over yourself. Not everything is about what you have or haven't done. Can you possibly just step back for once and see that where we are is about both of us? That I'm not putting you down or minimizing what you've provided, but questioning the choices we've both made."

Samantha paused to take a drink, maybe a mistake, she was feeling it now and that may go south quickly, this she knew from their years of arguing patterns. But she didn't care and she didn't dare stop now. She was determined to tell him what she thought.

"I don't regret one aspect of the actual life we built together, the children, our company, our friendships. What I question is that we never had an *"us"*. We moved so fast in the beginning, we never had the time to just be a couple, newlyweds, free. Have you forgotten that I got pregnant with Ashley just two months after we got married? Again, NO regrets there, but for us, as a couple, you have to agree that we got the short end there. And maybe . . . "

"Maybe what, Sam, maybe if we'd had more *"couple time"* as you put it, we wouldn't have done it at all?"

"Fuck you, Michael, that's not what I'm saying, you idiot."

"Oh, there you go, insult me, you get so fucking mean when you drink."

"Ha! Really? You're an ass, you're drinking, you're the one shouting, cussing, but it's me that gets mean?"

"You always have to put me down. I'm so sick of listening to how unfulfilled you are. You think you can do better, by all means, get the fuck out!" He waved his hand through the air across the garden.

"And here we are — AGAIN — I never said I wanted to leave or that I could do better. I'm asking you honest questions and you can't stand it. You like to float along, pretending everything is perfect and when it's not, it's someone else's issue because God forbid — you never do anything but work, provide, blah — blah — blah. What the fuck are we doing Michael, this is it. This is what we always get back to and . . . "

"And what, I don't care, I don't take you seriously. Sam, I'm so tired of trying for you. It's never enough. The money, the time, you are never satisfied."

"You're so full of shit, Michael. Except for the time, you may have that right. Especially the past year — right? You were busy with — oh yeah — fucking someone else."

Those words hit him hard. And she knew it, she had it right there, finally she had his full attention. He had no comeback, no insult, no idea what to say.

"Michael, you don't get to be the victim here. No matter how much you try and play the *"it was both of us"* card, you went the extra mile and now we get to figure it all out. Maybe . . . "

With that, Samantha stopped cold, got up, grabbed her drink and went inside. She could have kept going, she had so much more to say to him, but she took the road less travelled this time. Rather than tumble further down the rabbit hole, rather than repeat the patterns of the past, she opted to try something new. To step aside, give it all time to settle and to finish when they were both rested and sober. Assuming, of course, that he'd let her. Another pattern was that one of them would make the attempt to stop and the other just wouldn't let it go. To her surprise, he didn't follow her in. Grateful, she undressed, crawled into bed and began to read over her journal, hoping she'd find some ray of light under which to continue her journey here. She glanced up occasionally to see Michael still sitting at the table, staring upward to the sky. He looked peaceful, she thought, maybe she'd gotten through, maybe he was contemplating her words for a change instead of glossing over them. Maybe there was a chance for them.

After about an hour Michael strolled in from the patio, notably relaxed, "What's that you're reading?"

"Nothing."

Samantha closed the cover, slipping it back into the drawer of her nightstand. "Just going over my calendar and lists for the week. So many gifts to bring home this trip."

Secrets, she thought, *my voice and you don't get to hear it — any of it*. How easily deception rolled from her lips. Maybe they were more aptly matched than she cared to admit.

"Thank you for letting me be, Michael. I'm so tired of our fighting the way we have. I really do want to get to the bottom of us and see what that foundation looks like. I'm not so sure it's in the ruins you or I imagine it to be."

"God, Sam, exactly what I was thinking about out there. When did we stop listening to each other? When did we stop putting each other first?"

"I don't know, but I do know this: tonight could have ended as it always has and it didn't, so it might just mean that we are ready to start listening again."

"I love you more than anything in this world, Sam, let's figure this out."

"Well, we'll try right? That's a start." She turned off her light and rolled over, her back to him. "Good night, babe, tomorrow's gonna come soon enough. I need sleep. I do love you."

He sat on the bed beside her and watched her as she slipped off into sleep. "Tomorrow does come, Sam," he whispered to himself, hoping with all his heart that they could find a way back to each other.

"With **love,**

it's never really the last time.

The hope for one more chance

is always there, **burning**

just beneath the surface."

Florence, Italy

MONDAY, MARCH 13, 2017

Samantha woke to find Michael gone, a note on her nightstand.

> Didn't want to wake you baby, I'm off to meet Carlo at the Osmannoro site. Wish us luck. If all goes as planned we wrap it up today. Should be good for lunch at 1:30. Let me know where — I'll text if something changes.
>
> Love you~

"Well okay!" 7:00 a.m. — Samantha welcomed the morning to herself. She had so much catching up to do. Allegra, Kelly, she needed to speak to them both. She thought it odd that Kelly hadn't called her back yet, just not like her. She'd call her first. Invigorated, Samantha threw back the sheets and jumped to her feet. Coffee and fruit were waiting for her on the patio. There was a slight chill in the air, the grounds were quiet with only the birds singing. *What a beautiful start to the day*, she smiled. Samantha never tired of the setting. She relaxed back in her seat — feet on the adjacent chair and called her sister.

"Kelly! Where the hell have you been?"

She was so happy to hear her sister's voice.

"Jesus, Sam, it's almost midnight here, I hate this time difference. Where are you, how are you, did you tell Michael, what the fuck is going on over there?"

"Sit, sister, we have a lot of catching up to do."

Samantha spent the next 20 or so minutes filling her in on everything — Michael, Allegra, where her head was right now, which, she surprised herself as she spoke, was in a really calm place. Gone, at least for now, were the feelings of ineptness, confusion and anger that had plagued her for what seemed an eternity.

"No fucking way?! Thank God you listened to me and kept your big mouth shut." Kelly was, as always, dramatic and insistent. "Can you imagine if you'd spilled your guts to him first? Ha, now it's all on him, asshole. I have friends, I can bury that bastard, you know that right?!"

"Relax, sister, we are working through things. If we don't, I promise I'll let you know." Samantha laughed at their exchange, reminiscing about their relationship. It was a friendship stronger than bloodlines and it was rare, what she saw now between her own children. Kelly had an irreverence toward life that Samantha envied. As much of a free spirit as Sam fancied herself, Kelly was the one who got it. She took life one second at a time and lived the hell out of it. Irresponsibly, some would say, but through it all she lived her life her way, was loyal to her own detriment and usually had the last laugh.

"Seriously baby, I will take that mother-fucker down. He can't do this to you."

"Kelly, stop . . . it's okay I swear, we are together, figuring it all out. But you are right about one thing, I am so damned glad I let things play the way they have. I'm not ready to pull the trigger, maybe I never really was, and maybe that was the problem."

She was asking really, not sure of the answer.

"Samantha! Don't second guess yourself — EVVV-E-R!"

She exaggerated her enunciation, her trademark, to make sure her point was made.

"You have NOTHING to be sorry for. You live, my beautiful sister, and fuck anyone who gets in your way. I wish I were there, I just want to hug you. When will you see Allegra next? Are you sure she's telling you everything?"

Samantha recounted everything from that night, as best she could, welling up with tears, shaking as she spoke.

"So yeah, that's all I know, I'll talk with her later this morning. My plan right now is to fly home Thursday, then straight to LA to finish the work on Robert's graduation and fly back here, two weeks, I think. Yay! Short time in Dallas."

"Okay, well I'm here. I'll pick you up — let me know when you get in."

"I'll call you, but I'll have a car so don't worry. I'm staying at the Beverly Hills Hotel, come stay with me, it'll be fun."

"Of course you are! You have the life girl — and you should, you deserve everything, more of it now!"

Kelly laughed uncontrollably. She'd been so much for Samantha, sister, friend, mother to some extent and always her biggest cheerleader.

"And you're good? Why haven't you called, what's going on?"

Samantha asked, knowing full well what the answer would be and that the call would soon end. She would bury any negativity she faced, self-inflicted or otherwise. Kelly had never been able to face that music in her own world. She was far better suited to leading damage control for everyone around her than she was at putting out the fires constantly burning at her feet. Samantha hated that, Kelly would never let her help her, be there for her, be her cheerleader. Somewhere along the way she finally just stopped fighting it. It was easier and less disappointing. Samantha swallowed the acquiescence pill years ago. It had became her style of coping and as she sat on the patio in Florence that morning, she couldn't help wonder how it had failed her over the years. She could argue, and often did, that she only had herself to blame. Just accepting it all, too much, not enough, happy, sad, overjoyed, unfulfilled. She made lists, long ones, of her perceived shortcomings and habits in dealing with people and situations. Samantha realized that it wasn't just Kelly who refused to walk through the emotional tumult, she avoided it at all costs, too. But over these past months she was rediscovering her voice and the satisfaction that came from insisting it be heard.

"Oh yeah, fine, you know, same shit always, I'll tell you later when I have more time, I gotta run now. Love you to the moon."

Samantha smiled as she disconnected, watching the playful geese across the yard waking up with the rest of the world. She contemplated their conversation and the one thing that resonated was that she truly did believe her words. She and Michael were on their way to a good place, good enough anyway, and ready to try again. Samantha dialed up Allegra, only to get her voicemail, so she left a quick message, read emails, scrolled through social media pages, then jumped in the shower, relaxed and ready to get on to her day. The sun was working tirelessly to break through the low hanging clouds. There was a peculiar tint to the sky, not a storm-coming kind of grey, more of a metallic blue, mixed up with charcoal and gold. Like sheets of glass — reflecting the world around her. *Weird,* she thought as she watched the clouds, *everything, everywhere, everyone around me is a contradiction. Not even the rain is sure it wants to come out and play.* She laughed at the image those thoughts conjured up. Neptune with his Triton dancing across the sky taunting the other Gods . . .

"Oh my gosh!" Samantha screeched, it was already noon and she wanted to take a good, long walk before meeting Michael. "Where did the morning go?"

Just then Fausto rang, "Signora, there is a package here for you in the lobby, it is quite large, can you please come to claim it before we bring it over."

"Of course, thank you. I'll be right there."

The timing of the call was great, but a large package? Samantha was curious, what could it possibly be? She gathered her things quickly, anxious to find out. The lobby was quiet. Monday, she guessed as she looked up and across the foyer to see Michael, a picnic basket on the ground next to him, holding five sunflowers. She marveled at the sight. Her favorite flower. The ritual had started simply enough when she'd mentioned that to him the summer they met. One turned into two, eventually to five, representing their family. She couldn't remember the last time he'd done it. *Oh, how you can charm when you want to,* she thought. Samantha smiled as she walked up to him, taking the blooms from his extended arm, which he gently wrapped around her waist pulling her in for a kiss. She wrestled with the emotions rolling through her, trying desperately not to give in to the questions and insecurities hovering just beneath the surface. She'd long been the recipient of Michael's doting charms and attention — she tried not to picture his efforts to woo "*her*" — the "*other woman*". But the images kept coming. *No!* she admonished herself, *stop — just be here now, fuck her — fuck him for fucking her.* And as her comedic inner dialogue took over, she smiled outwardly and kissed Michael back, long and hard.

"Nice touch, cowboy. I thought you were in Sesto all morning."

"Tomorrow. Went in to the office instead to finish the contracts with Carlo and the lawyers, it's done baby, we got it all, two parcels behind IKEA, and the three farms just northwest across the autostrada. Carlo hit a home run, no question."

They'd been working on this for over a year and she could see the relief and exuberance on his face. It was indeed a home run, the farms would be cultivated into a sustainable, luxury resort — they were leading the way into new territory for the agritourismo market and this concept was Michael's vision from the beginning. Their company built its portfolio early on, investing in existing properties throughout

Italy, but this was Michael's dream. He'd envisioned the big picture early on, but it had been slow to materialize. Another of his enviable strengths — patience. He waited and worked tirelessly to bring all the elements together at a time when they and the market were ready for it. While it followed the current industry model of a sustainable, working farm offering lodging and a variety of experiences and amenities, adding the five-star luxury accommodation and property aspect was a strong departure. "Upping the ante, broadening the market," he'd tell her, "we'll have it all." He was passionate and believed completely that this was the future. Once that mindset kicked in, there was no stopping him. He'd spent the last six years singly focused on making this happen. She was happy to see his hard work and dreams coming to fruition, though it was going to be a long road ahead — for both of them. It hit her almost the minute he said it, this would tie them into the area for years to come. He'd be in Italy more than usual. She couldn't be happier for that. Fuck it, she thought, time to be here and California full-time — a seamless, natural departure from that God-awful place she currently called home.

As if reading her mind, he said, "Sam, this is just the start, there is a lot of groundwork to lay here. Don't get ahead of yourself."

"Fuck off!" She elbowed him, laughing, knowing full well that it would take time. But she would stay ahead of it, planning her *"escape"* as she often referred to any Dallas departure.

"You do realize that the universe is on our side right now, you get that right?" she said.

She threw it out there, caution to the wind, her insight and belief that the universe and her angels were always with her.

"I do babe, I have no other explanation really. Friday, at dinner, Carlo was so far off on our numbers, there was no way I saw this happening as seamlessly as it has today. So maybe there is something to all your voodoo shit."

"Not voodoo or shit, schmuck!"

Her voice was warm and adoring, he was making the effort, all she really ever wanted from him. He didn't need to walk it with her, just respect her journey and believe in her.

"It's all out there, Michael, everything we want, what we wish for. Our intent. Every single event and interaction these past three days has brought us here, and, I believe with all my heart it has done so much to move us forward together." Samantha was taken aback by the ease of that word, together. She wanted to be here with him.

He picked up the the basket, kissed her forehead, wove his fingers through hers, tightly gripped her hand and led her through the lobby out onto the cobblestone walkway along Borgo Pinti.

"Walk with me, Sam, stay with me . . . "

His voice was a bit shaky, but just as amiable. He was walking on air, she sensed, and fell in step with him. He seemed confident and optimistic that they were taking the steps to heal, that she would stay with him and forgive him. Eyeing the sun changing the tones of his hair as it tousled about with each step, she took stock of the man. Damn, he still turned her on, his khaki shorts and turquoise pullover were as sexy from the rear as ever. Samantha could envision their future together. She saw them as one again — a couple — a partnership, stronger this time around if they could put the last five years behind them. She tilted her head up, toward the sun, letting Michael's hand guide her, and in that instant she felt it. His balmy fingers rolling across hers, entangling their palms. She didn't want to make this walk with anyone else. She could leave, now she certainly had more cause to, but that's not at all what the beats in her heart were urging. Her gaze swept slowly down his back, watching him as they strolled, making their way through Il Centro toward the Arno. The early afternoon breeze off the river was cool, he stopped her just to the south of the Ponte Vecchio. She felt it too, what was welling up inside him.

"Sam, I can't go back. I can't un-hurt you. But I can promise you that I will spend every minute of every day trying. Trying to make us right again." He lowered his head, eyes closed, "if you'll let me. Please let me. Please, Sam, let me." His lips grazed her ear as he whispered his pleas.

Samantha grasped his jaw with her free hand, turning it downward, in line with her eyes, wide open, looking deeply into his, her words smiled as she spoke. "Michael, you may be a cheating whore, but you're my cheating whore." Her tenor lightened the mood for them both. "We're not so terribly different, you know. I came here to leave you, well, to suggest a break."

Fuck! She hadn't been ready to say those words out loud, she thought, but apparently they were ready to be spoken and there was no turning back now. Michael's expression changed, he was stunned with her admission.

"I was tired of pretending, we hadn't worked for a long

time. We just kept going through the motions, surface shit — I hate that."

She dropped her hand, wrapping both arms around his waist, looking up to him, much as she had the first time he held her not far from where they stood today. *A lifetime ago,* she thought as she continued, "But when you told me what you'd done, as sick as this sounds, I loved you more — after I decided not to kill you, of course!" She smiled. "You were finally being honest, real with me. I'm not fragile, I don't need you to protect me. We do this together or we don't do it at all. It's not you I wanted to leave, it's the empty stereotype we've become. I just can't be that person anymore."

"C'mon," Michael took her hand and walked toward the Ponte Vecchio. "Let's walk, looks like it might really rain. Beautiful, isn't it?"

Samantha watched the clouds gathering above as she continued, "I can't even fathom this relationship you've had this past year, I . . . "

"Sam, I ended it, I want you — I want us. I fucked it all up."

"You did."

The corner of her lips parted, a slight grin, she held the cards, it felt good. "We're going to Boboli, aren't we?"

"Yup."

"Perfect! Remember the day after our wedding?"

"Of course, that's why I planned this. We snuck away, early that morning, you took me there to *"talk"*. You always made such a production of *"talking"*. Why was it so hard for you?"

"I don't know. But I thought about that when I was

talking to Kelly this morning. We just always avoided the *"hard stuff"*. So when you came along, with your, *"we talk about everything"* mode, it wasn't so easy for me, you know?"

"What I know is that you eventually came around, I just suffered through the waiting for it!"

"Yeah, well, I did plenty of suffering too. You're no walk in the park yourself!"

They spent the 20-minute walk to the Gardens reminiscing, joking, recalling why they'd fallen in love in the first place. It felt new to Samantha, they were there, together, making the effort to get back to who they were before life had its way with them and she liked it. More so, she believed it. They had been little more than strangers marrying, living out their days, were they waiting for the real thing to come along? Had they simply settled? No! There was a much deeper connection and she felt it today, strong — present. This was no longer just about finding her way to happiness, the story had changed these past days. The question now was could they begin again — with each other. So many friends she'd watched face this very fork in the road — watched them opt out — leave it all behind — start over — shiny and new. And who was she to judge anyone? But as she walked with Michael now, today — his hand in hers — it was becoming crystal clear to her that she liked, no, she loved who they were when they started out. And just maybe they could get back there and keep building what they'd started so many years before. But they'd need to acknowledge that it may look dramatically different than either of them had imagined. Maybe the way out, the way to unfettered happiness would come from not leaving, but from staying. From facing the struggle together and in that effort and commitment they might find their happily ever after. Maybe . . . .

"Shit!" Michael stopped as they approached the entrance to the gardens.

"The picnic basket?" Sam responded.

He just shook his head and started laughing. "I left it back at the bridge, Goddamnit."

"Oh, who cares," Sam comforted. "Less to carry, let's go, we'll eat afterwards. I remember the first time I brought you here. You were so NOT into any of it."

Samantha laughed at the memory. Michael had gone along for the stroll begrudgingly. He'd never been a picnic-in-the-park kind of guy. Today, he seemed to relish every step.

"Oh God, I remember too. I wanted to be with you, so I walked, and walked, and walked."

The two of them knocked each other about joyfully recalling the afternoon. Winding through the acres of the Boboli, Samantha's escape of choice.

The 11 acres of Niccolo Pericoli's sixteenth-century landscape design masterpiece had become a sanctuary, offering refuge from the storms life sent her way. It was at the same time a playground. Even its name made her smile. She could get lost in spirit and body wandering the cypress covered footpaths, the steps from the amphitheater taking her to Neptune's Fountain. The irony of her vision earlier that morning, Neptune playing in the sky, made the hair on her arms rise. And then there were the rose beds. When describing his life at Laurentum, Pliny the Younger said the purpose of a garden was to offer serenity and peace. Samantha made a point, still, to visit the gardens in spring when the bright pink roses were in full bloom. They brought the memory of her mother to life. She found hope and comfort in those petals. Today was no different. She paused as they passed, fragrant rows of new beginnings entangled with every memory she held in her heart. One more example to ponder — the yin and the yang of her existence presently. "*Let It Be*", her Mom's words drifted through her, causing her to smile.

Michael responded unwittingly, "I'm happy, too, baby. God this feels good."

"Yes, it feels right. So right." His voice lured her back to the present and it did feel good, nowhere near done though, no easy road ahead, she was sure of that, but the connection she felt was genuine and simply recognizing that was a huge milestone for them.

They spent the next hour winding about the maze, ducking behind trees, embracing, kissing, love reborn. Samantha considered the prospect that she'd have to get to a place of really moving beyond his infidelity. Then there'd be the challenges of behavior that got them there in the first place. No amount of sex and newness would totally change that, for either of them. Though she firmly believed she'd evolved to a stronger place than she'd found herself in five years earlier. He'd either be on board with those changes in her and what that meant, to how they evolved as a couple, or not. Pretty simple, she figured, but all in good time.

"Sam, did you hear me?"

No, she'd been lost in her thoughts, contemplating their future, she wanted to tell him.

"We gotta get back, this is a good-size storm coming."

She didn't have to ask, sprinkles turning into drops fell on her. *Ahhhh the rains — perfect.* Another a sign, she was sure of it.

"I love you, Michael."

Samantha stood still, not a care in the world as the rain and winds picked up, soaked and laughing. Michael pulled her behind one of the larger trees, kissing her, slowly, deeply, breathing hope into her. He tried to lift her, taking one hand underneath her.

"Don't," she admonished him, playfully. "Don't."

"I can't help it. Blame it on the rain, baby."

He'd settle for passionate kisses right now.

"Song?"

Sam didn't answer directly, rather she whispered two lines from Fleetwood Mac's "Storm".

"I've never been a blue calm sea, I've always been a storm."

"You?"

"I Won't Ever Give Up."

"Really . . . ."

Surprised by his choice, she asked, "Jason Mraz? That's an intriguing departure."

"Hey! I may not know lyrics like you do, but give me a little credit. I heard it this morning and couldn't have said it any better — like they were written for me."

Wrinkled nose, his smile shone through the rain.

"Well I won't give up on us, even if the skies get rough." Samantha knew it well. "That's it! Exactly — see I can reach . . . "

Michael was happy to meet her on this level of the appreciation she had for the connection of life and lyrics.

"Yes, you can darlin', yes you can." Samantha mirrored his demeanor.

The storm's intensity and hunger pangs took center stage, they ran most of the way back toward Il Centro, stepping into Trattoria Ponte Vecchio after crossing the bridge. Michael ordered a bottle of Amarone as he nestled into a window seat. Samantha sat down next to him. What she mulled over as they waved about their napkins in the futile exercise of drying each other, was the the amount of talking they'd engaged in these past days. More substance, more fun, more real, she concluded, than they had seen in ages. She thought about the saying *"a garden grows best where you water it"*. Their drought, self- inflicted as it may be, appeared to be coming to an end. The landscape was changing, their dialogue was changing. Life, Samantha acknowledged, was changing right in front of her — for her — because of her. She looked up from her wine, into Michael's eyes. She was home.

Samantha grabbed her purse, she said "Bathroom — definitely order me a Margherita pizza, anything else is fine." Michael watched her glide across the room. How could he possibly have ever thought he might let this go — slip through his fingers? He'd lost sight of what they'd had. They were much better together than they could ever be on their own. That was clear as his gaze followed her, remembering the girl he'd lost his heart to right here. It seemed like yesterday. He shook his head, lifted his glass, and made a silent toast, *To Sam.* She was different, he had to admit that he was intrigued. The very traits that he'd been fighting in her for a long time had metamorphosed. She was more self-assured and seemingly happy with herself than he could recall. Most notably, he admitted, he liked it. She was evolving into an independent, strong and outspoken woman.

Michael placed their order as he watched her disappear down the hallway.

"Maybe we are the **statistics,**

the rule rather than the exception

and **accepting** that is the

real challenge."

Florence, Italy

MONDAY, MARCH 13, 2017

Deep in thought, Michael's eyes lingered on the empty hallway, even after Samantha had disappeared around the corner. Sipping wine, imagining her there, alone in the bathroom, he pictured her naked body next to his earlier in the day. He had to admit, he just may have pulled the get out of jail free card every man needs at one time or another. He'd fucked up, he'd owned up and from where he sat now it seemed he'd ended up back on top. Okay, not so much on top — just not out of the game altogether. That was an image he could enjoy. He and Sam were both so competitive, she'd appreciate the analogy, he was sure of it. "All of life's games, the wins, the losses — don't let them get the best of you," he'd tell her. "Make the best of them and you'll always win." That thought froze on his lips — could their entire life together really be reduced to the innocuous meanderings of a never-ending game? Did they subconsciously keep score of each other's successes and failures toward each other? He was pretty sure Sam did. She let little slip by unnoticed. She may not mention it or act upon a violation but she would most definitely never forget it. And, now that he brought it up, he'd have to agree that he did as well. He kept score, she hurt him, she ignored him, she loved him, she didn't. There were tallies, years of mental note taking. What he'd ever planned to do with the accumulation he couldn't say. What he could say to himself today was that none of it mattered — none of it fucking mattered.

What mattered was that he was there with her again, loving her again, hoping for a future with her again. That was why you played the game, why you fought to win at any cost. Love and friendship. Connecting with the one human being on the planet that makes you laugh and cry with equal intensity was the reason for living. The one who alway brings you back to who you are — shines the mirror on you, reflecting your very heart and soul. It is the stuff dreams are made of. *How,* he wondered, *did I lose that when clearly I am lost without it? Why chance it, why not battle every minute to keep it close and safe? And why in the hell did I ever consider letting someone else walk in and take it away?* In that moment of conjecture he realized how Sam must have felt when he told her about his affair. How it must have burned as the spear pierced her heart. Hearing him utter those three words, "I met someone." Did she feel he was overtly trying to replace her or just satisfy his ego? He suspected it was a bit of both, but he couldn't possibly know exactly what ran through her mind as he said it. He saw the pain in her eyes. Sam wore her heart openly on her sleeve, on her face, in her voice and it screamed at him that night. He watched anger replace hurt. He watched in deafening silence as Sam tried to put the pieces together in her head. Not talking, he'd even wished she'd struck out at him.

Then, slowly it came. Through actions, their talking and being together — seriously being together. Maybe they were both afraid to let go for fear it would slip through their fingers and be gone forever. And there they'd be, at the cliff's edge, paralyzed voyeurs watching eternity fade into the distance. There was definitely an urgency to their togetherness these past three days. If he was feeling it, so was she. He'd ask her about that later, there was still so much work to be done. He was up for it, ready for it, ready for Sam — all of it. Michael took a good swig of his wine, and gazed around the restaurant, which was still fairly empty. He tossed his napkin on the table, and found his way down the hall. He stood outside the bathroom, mindlessly rubbing his fingertips over the doorknob. What was he doing, he shook his head, absently massaging the three-day-old scruff along his jawline. *God! Has it only been three days?* He was still awed by that glaring fact. He lifted his hand and stepped back from the door. Here they were, just 72 hours beyond his late night confession. What had he been thinking? Telling Sam the way he did, blurting it out as if telling her the score of a football game. Taking a deep breath and spitting out to her that he'd been unfaithful, had broken every promise they'd ever made to each other, in wedded bliss or otherwise. Ending it just hours earlier with a good fuck to ease the blow. Not just one night, but months of *"one nights"* that had become more than he'd ever intended. He hardly recognized himself. Who the hell was he?

It wasn't planned, these things never are — the chance meeting that flips your world upside down. You don't wake up one morning and think, 'yeah, it's a good day to light up my life.' And yet, that is exactly what happened. Strangers meeting in a bar, canyons of emptiness filled with conversation, sparks, attraction, energy — telling yourself it's okay, just this once — no harm, no foul. But one night turns into the next morning, into casual meetings, into the intricately woven lies you tell yourself to justify what you're doing. The lies upon lies that make living with the truth bearable. Suddenly you're living two lives, spinning a growing web of deceit and broken promises. Still convinced that it won't end badly for anyone because that had never been your intention, it just happened.

I'm not taking the whole hit here, but I will take the sole responsibility for crossing the line we said we wouldn't. Sam and I had often talked openly about life, marriage, relationships and the in-betweens, vowing never to allow momentary indiscretions to jeopardize what we had. In other words, one night, maybe — a relationship, never. But that's exactly what happened and it's not so black and white. In theory it all works, the idea, the promises. Then suddenly it doesn't, it all gets dirty, it all changes. We were off, we had been for months. Sam had checked out, emotionally and physically. Don't get me wrong — she was an unbelievable mother — the reason that our kids are who they are today. But she'd stopped being my wife somewhere along the way. We stopped being a couple, instead we'd become two people sharing real estate, connected on paper, in name. That was about it. I finally understood the "going through the motions" picture so many of my friends painted as they attempted to define the evolution of their own broken marriages. I just never thought it would happen to us.

Sam and I began our life together as partners in every way. But the reality was far from that — we had a great physical connection, humor, conversation. Sam was smart, independent, feisty and strong-willed, absolutely one of the biggest turn-ons for me. But partners, let's be honest, what does that mean, the scales were tipped. We defined our roles within our marriage early on and it worked well. She managed our home, the kids, our social calendar. I built the company, our financial security and at the end of the day there was no partnership there. If I stopped, so did our income stream — along with the life she'd come to enjoy. I don't want to say she took it for granted, but she'd come to expect that it would always be there. And lately, less tolerant of the work I had to do to keep it all together, less forgiving and more demanding. At least that's how it felt, really since the kids began their successive departures.

Sam changed — it all changed. Slowly, but I can't put my finger on any one day or incident where I became aware of the actual shift. I know she was struggling, but she would never really talk about how and why. For fuck's sake, she had one hell of an enviable life. The life that I still worked around the clock to provide. I held the goddamned door open for her entrée into the 3-comma club and she was sure as hell all about that and everything that came with it. It was me she didn't seem to need anymore. Her "partnering" had taken on a life of its own — boards, tennis buddies, activities that took more and more of her attention and time, not leaving much of anything for me. And what about me? She seemed to enjoy reminding me often who I really was, according to her, that I wasn't "all that". I know exactly who I am, where I came from. The kid who grew up in Manhattan, just this side of privilege. The one who watched from afar, who studied, worked and moved to achieve it. Who was Sam to judge me from the only Dallas address she would consider, her Turtle Creek estate. The one my sweat and stress built. She treated me like the guy at the Uffizi — still on his way up, not there yet. Well, I was there, and I'd worked my ass off to get us there, I deserved that respect and attention, or so I told myself. That somehow legitimized the women clambering to give it to me. Even though I didn't act on the constant advances, I have to admit they felt good. But then last summer I met her, and every single thing I thought I had been missing came raining down. I felt alive again, desirable, wanted, needed — hell, appreciated. Here I was, succumbing to all those egotistical attributes we chastise in others as we watch them desperately clinging to their youth, aching to find something new, something better. She didn't expect or assume I'd provide anything, she just wanted to be with me. We laughed, we talked, and we had un-fucking-believable sex.

Sex with Sam had become obligatory, a "drive-by", unimaginative, predictable, all the while pretending it didn't matter. But it did, I was lonely and angry. So it was easy to start spending more time in Florence. The business was growing so fast. Over the past three years, Carlo could have easily handled the Italian investments, but I made it my responsibility to be there. I stayed away longer and longer until I felt out of sorts back in Dallas. As I spent more time in Italy, I found it easy to vindicate my marital departure, to excuse any bad behavior

I engaged in. After all, I wasn't needed at home and frankly I didn't feel wanted there. Sam seemed to be settling into her life with the kids gone and she made little effort to include me when I was there. I just didn't fit in anymore. I didn't care for her new friends. I felt like the only sober one at the party — there physically but just not "getting" any of it — the proverbial "outsider". I'd become an inconvenience. We talked only as much as we needed to. Giving my attention to my life in Florence became easier and easier — happier I hate to say, but it was true. I looked forward to each return and dreaded leaving. I was no longer going home. It wasn't home — it was a place I lived with a woman I'd loved once but didn't know anymore — wasn't sure I even wanted anymore.

It makes sense when I say it like this — viewing the past five years through these eyes of deceit. It was all a fucking lie. The one we tell ourselves over and over. The one we pretend won't hurt anyone, because we believe we deserve to be happy again, no matter the cost. I convinced myself that I was different, but really, not so much. I took the easy way out and God it was so much easier — no wading through the contemptuous years that got you to this point. Just close the door, shut out the past and bask in the present — the woman in front of you — no baggage, no history — excited by who and what you are. I told myself that it mattered. That she understood me. That she got me, and that we could be happy. Making excuses every step of the way — and the lies . . . God, the lies. One after the other, building higher walls with every absurd tale, believing that I'd earned the right to be happy and since I wasn't, it was all good. Until it wasn't. I actually believed I was doing us all a favor. The only real favor came last week, when Stefania threatened me. That betrayal of friendship and love, her ultimatum — "tell her or I will". Her words still haunt me. Goddammit, they pierced my soul. My ego, most certainly. Game over — look in the mirror Michael — no way out. Now I can't believe I might actually thank her for pushing me to the ledge. I mean look at us now — three days — lifetime. Starting over, I think . . .

Michael brushed his fingers through his hair, raised his head, smiled and reached for the doorknob. Age had taken its toll on the lock, with just a slight struggle it flung open, smacking the sink behind. He glanced over his shoulder to see that no one else was headed his way, walked in and latched the door's chain behind him, glad Sam hadn't seen the need for that extra measure. He could hear her rustling about as he persuaded the fragile stall door to open. Her vulnerability exposed a natural beauty he'd lost sight of in recent years. She looked up at him, distraught, at first, discomfort replaced by ease as her eyes made their way up and down his frame. He was confident she'd welcome his intrusion — but she hesitated, causing him to question his decision. Had he pushed to far, too soon? Adolescent nerves shot through him, he leaned back against the stall's door, eyes locked on hers, waiting — hoping for some sort of welcome gesture. What he saw as hesitation was Samantha taking in the love standing in front of her. Re-playing every minute of the past three days, now soaking in the pleasure of where they'd come, addressing the fear of where they may end up. Michael stood, paralyzed, waiting for a word or action from her. She just stared, seeing him as the self-assured man she'd fallen for a lifetime ago with no idea of the anxiety consuming him — staring silently back at her. They danced — without words, without movement — sizing each other up, there in the tiny, antiquated bathroom stall, raindrops pinging the window behind them.

It all came to a head of sorts, there and then — they'd each arrived in the moment with their own agenda, certain the choices they had made were for the best. And it seemed that perhaps that is exactly what was happening.

"Hi," Samantha finally whispered with a smile. Michael moved in, no more waiting or wondering.

"Babe." His adrenaline railed through him, he nearly lifted her off the ground, kissing her as if his life depended on it. In some ways it did, he guessed. Given where they'd come since Friday night — it all could have taken so many different turns, and likely would over the next days, months, years, if they were committed to working through it.

She caught him off balance, releasing his belt and unzipping his shorts, letting them fall to the ground. Exposed, Michael gasped, relief and release. Samantha kneeled and took him in her mouth, he closed his eyes, extended his arms bracing himself against the stall door and let go. Their sweat permeated the room, jumbled passions, pain, and joy consumed each of them, swaying together as he reached an ecstatic climax. Silence washed over each of them, lost in their own thoughts, Samantha looked up at Michael, head resting against the door, his arms gripping her shoulders, *peaceful*, she thought, *spent, even*. She empathized with the sight, feeling it too — sheer exhaustion — letting it all flow out — finally.

Michael spoke softly, guiding her up to kiss her once more. "God, I love the fuck out of you."

"Stop talking — just kiss me!" she whispered.

His head bobbed back and forth as if searching for words that just didn't need to be said. His eyes did the talking, glowing, teary, though clear with intent. She believed him, he wanted to make this relationship work, she could feel the ache in his heart, radiating through her as they stood motionless, staring at each other. Michael broke the spell, leaned down, pulled up his shorts, kissed her forehead and turned to leave.

"You know, a gentleman would've fucked me right back in here." Her voice filled with laughter.

"Ha! Well, a gentleman wouldn't have had you on your knees in a public stall — but you got me baby."

"I do, and we've got this, I think." She grabbed his ass once more. "Go on, I'll be right out."

Samantha pulled herself together, stood in front of the mirror, praying for just a few minutes of privacy. She barely recognized her reflection peering at her though the cracked glass. There she was again — the young girl she'd left behind, the vulnerable child she'd tucked away as she began to navigate the strange waters hoping to build a life for herself all alone. The disturbing recollection of the reflection she saw in the storefront window in Venice. She thought about the volumes of mistakes she'd made along the way, the wrong turns, wasted efforts, broken dreams. And yet, through it all, she'd managed to do exactly what she'd hoped she might — make a family. Be part of something bigger than she ever could be on her own. Slowly tucking her shirt in, wiping away the mascara trailing its way down her cheek, Sam allowed herself a smile, confirmation that she and Michael had created a beautiful life and this legacy would not have a broken ending. Not if she could help it.

"Jeez, how long were we in there?" Samantha nudged Michael as she scooted her chair closer to him. The sky had darkened, heavy raindrops now falling, rippling across the river's surface, the tables had filled, an electric energy surged throughout the cafe. They talked, eating and drinking as only one does in Florence, slowly engaged in the present. Nowhere to go, nowhere to be.

Hours later, the magic light of the Duomo called to them as they strolled through the old city. Brunelleschi's masterpiece — Santa Maria del Fiore — built nearly six centuries earlier, was a source of peace for Samantha. Michael appreciated the connection she spoke of, though it was far removed from his own. But that was her, the vantage point from which she approached life — searching for deeper meaning to it all. Charming, Michael had often felt, but tonight he saw it through her eyes. They stopped at the front entrance across from the Baptistry. Samantha took his hand in hers, not a word between them. The creation of the dome set off the Renaissance. To this day the success of his design is still shrouded in mystery.

Sam was thinking about that as she admired the magnificent structure in front of her, still the largest masonry dome on the planet. The inspiration and the details of the work he did to create his design followed the intensely private Brunelleschi to his grave. Sam appreciated that, maybe too much. *Not everything we do or think in this life needs to be shared.* Words she held close to her heart, most especially today. *Secrets — sometimes a good thing. Sometimes a very good thing.* Samantha pulled Michael's hand and began walking back to the hotel. The day was about as close to perfection as she could imagine. Only three days from now she would head back to Dallas, that was both saddening and surprising to her. She'd come here to leave, and here she was, longing to stay. Stay with Michael, stay the course, see it through. It would be painful, erratic and unpredictable. But she honestly thought this was the right move. At least it felt right — right now, and that had always worked for her.

"Life is a **constant process**

of editing our stories,

always hoping to

'get it right.'"

Florence, Italy

MONDAY, MARCH 13 – TUESDAY, MARCH 14, 2017

"Michael," Samantha tapped his shoulder. He'd moved to the patio, breathing in the storm's waning elixir. There had been so much said, yet so many feelings and questions still hung in the air, weighing her down. She wanted to talk. First she kissed him, garnering strength from his lips to open her own and hold nothing back.

"Michael?"

He turned to her as she handed him a glass of Macallan, clinking the one in her hand as she did, nodding, "sipping mood." Her tone was questioning, the prelude of things to come. He saw it in her eyes, the moment he'd been dreading, hoping maybe it wouldn't come, knowing full well it would, and that he'd have to give her answers. The thought of hurting her any more tugged at him, but he couldn't take his eyes off her. He'd rather run, instead, he sat down across from her and clasped her free hand into his. A comforting gesture for them both, touching seemed the surest way to stay connected. *Hold on, don't let go, no matter what, don't let her go.*

"How? Tell me how you met, tell me when, tell me where. Let's start there." She took a deep breath.

Michael lowered his head, rubbed his fingers through hers and in a barely audible voice peeled off the band-aid, slowly at first, answering only what she asked. He'd considered all the options long before this moment and the scenario that seemed the most honest, the least painful, was to answer only the questions she asked. Tenuously plodding over the memories, sharing details of the intimate, romantic relationship he'd had this past year, with his wife, the whole thing was ludicrous. He'd keep the secrets with him, where she didn't ask for explanations, telling her what he could to satisfy her curiosity without ramming it down her throat. Keep out as much emotion as he could, give her just the facts to provide the closure she could live with. This, he decided, would deliver the least painful blow. Time would tell, and the time had come. *Find the words Michael — you owe her that.*

"We met last summer in Rome. I had a board meeting at the de Russie, we met in the bar there . . . drinks, we danced . . . "

Blah blah blah — white noise . . . stop talking . . . Samantha watched his lips moving as she struggled to stop the spinning in her head. She knew exactly where they'd met. She and Michael had stayed there often. A clear picture was forming and Samantha wanted no part of it. She'd asked for this, but she wasn't so sure that she really wanted all the details. She wouldn't ask her name, she just couldn't put a name to her, not yet. If she didn't know her name, it made it less real, if that was even possible at this point.

Ridiculous, she knew that, but she got to be ridiculous here, this wasn't her story. *Ridiculous, now there's a level of irony I hadn't considered.* Samantha clenched her jaw. She was not completely innocent. He'd come to her, admitted infidelity, and was now genuinely working to right his multitude of wrongs. Commendable, she acknowledged, regardless of how he got to this soul-baring moment, this spiritual cleansing. At least he was trying. She, on the other hand, was perfectly content taking her secrets to the grave. It was a fine line to walk. She had no reason to confess anything. She'd kept their foolish promises, he hadn't. She couldn't fault him to the extent that she wanted to, couldn't punish him, couldn't hate any more. Anymore than she hated herself and that was enough.

"It wasn't much at first . . . Ca–"

"Stop!" Snapping back to the conversation, she realized he was about to say her name. Samantha reached over and cradled his jaw. "It's enough Michael, I don't want to know all the details and I don't want to know her name. At least not now, maybe never . . . "

Her voice trailed off, shaking. There were tears streaming down her cheeks.

"I don't want to do this Michael. I don't want to hear about you and her and love in Italy. Your year of living dangerously."

She laughed at that. *Good to know I still can,* she thought.

"I decided the night you told me that I wouldn't leave, not because of this. I would try to get past it, no one is perfect, no *thing* is perfect, but for the most part, for most our time together, it's been pretty close. So, I decided then that if you were honest about having ended it and about wanting to make our marriage a priority, I would be too."

Michael tried to speak.

"Wait, I'm not done. What I can't wrap my head around is how to go about it all. The roller coaster — I'm all over the place — with you, laughing, great sex, fun — then just like that I see or hear something that sends me back down the rabbit hole. I think about what you two did together, what sex was like, do you think of her when we are together, what does she look like — and please, don't tell me, I'm not looking for answers here. I guess what I am looking for is something you can't give me and I sure as fuck can't give myself — an ending. When it won't hurt, when I won't question it all, when I won't get sick to my stomach imagining you with her. I want it to stop and it won't — what if it never does?"

Michael kneeled on the wet stones between them, wrapping both arms around her waist,

"Song?"

Oh God, that was the last thing she wanted to do right now. But it did change the somber tone of the night, she smirked and shook her head . . .

"Landslide."

"Ouch"

"You asked! And you?"

"Wasted Time."

"Ahhhh, ok, hmmm." She closed her eyes and sighed.

"Sammie, I wish I could tell you when it all goes away, I wish I could make it all go away. Better yet, I wish I'd never done this to us to begin with. You do realize that we've talked more openly and more often in the past three days than we have in the past three years?"

"I know and that feels really good, I gotta tell you. I'm liking getting out of my head!"

"Ha! I'm liking it too, less guesswork for me."

"Fuck you, how often were you really listening to me, I mean beyond the superficial BS."

"Sam, why do you think I wasn't listening to you? I mean, come on!"

"Why, Michael? Because you incessantly talk *for* me, *at* me, not *to* me. So I . . . "

"Ok, maybe to some extent, but how often did you just, go, do, leave me out of the fold?"

Samantha let out a heavy sigh, and said, "Maybe more than I'd like to admit. Fuck!" She collapsed into him, slipping deliberately from her seat onto his lap, sobbing with a slight dose of laughter. He followed suit. Neither noticed the rain's encore, heavier, the lightning in the distance that lit up the sky.

"So for tonight, for right now — I believe we can heal. I don't for one minute believe that this is it. That we will just roll on — leave the past in the dust. But for now, you've got my heart and my promise to try. Now take the rest of me."

She wanted to make love, not the frenzied, urgent fucking they'd engaged in the past three days. She wanted to feel him, love him. She stood up, reached for his hand and led him inside to get exactly what she wanted — all of him.

Through the night, in the distant shadows of the moonlight, raindrops drowning out their tears and moans, they made love. Samantha reveled in the pure, raw pleasure of it all. She knew this was a turning point. There'd be many more, no doubt, each one laying foundation for the next as they attempted to rebuild their relationship. As they lay tangled in each other, exploring each other, as if for the first time, she felt the magnitude of the moment. Her fingers traced his body, touching his soul, she thought, *the scars we carry, the ones we see, the ones we keep buried deep within us, the ones we transmit unwittingly to those we love most. We are covered in layers of anguish, trying to shed the pain anyway we can — and it is always justified.* She flipped, rolling onto her side, spooning into him — he wrapped his arms around her, inching himself closer. In sync with the slow tempo of his heart beat against her back, it felt like home. That was the best way she could explain it — she finally felt like she was home. That would suffice for now, it was more than enough to quash the uncertainty winding through her. *Breathe girl — just breathe.* She smiled, took his hands into hers, and let nature's soundtrack lull her to sleep.

"There is purpose to the **madness**

and somewhere along the way,

it all **begins** to make sense."

Florence, Italy

TUESDAY, MARCH 14, 2017

"I don't get it, Sam — what the hell is it with bathroom sex?"

Kelly called just as Samantha was heading out for a stroll, alone for the day. Michael had left early to meet Carlo.

"You kill me! Don't get me wrong, I've done my share of it — but I just don't get the turn on."

They laughed and laughed. Her call, she lied, was just to check up on Samantha, but she soon fell into sharing what had been troubling her. Boyfriend, living arrangements, job. Poor Kelly, Samantha worried, *will you ever be content — I doubt it.*

"Hey, sis, gotta run, get to work — some of us do that! Love you to the moon."

"Bye. I'll call when I'm on my way to LA. Can't wait to see you." Samantha picked up her pace, the energy in the old city bordered frenetic this morning, she didn't want to miss a second of its beauty. Today was the kind of day that ignited creative composition. These were the hours that inspired Vivaldi's "Four Seasons", that urged artists to sit down to a blank canvas, writers to write, dancers to dance. She couldn't put into words the current of emotions surging through her. She was certain of this, the trajectory was up — in feeling, in doing — all upward. Samantha smiled, fending off the urge to raise her arms to the heavens. She was so happy, so content in the moment and it was enough. Spring had most definitely arrived, the streets were full. Shop owners were opening for the day, the intoxicating aroma of freshly baked breads wafted about, following her — its stream encircling her as she walked, leading her to stop in for a pastry and espresso. While satiating her cravings, she breathed in the totality of her surroundings, basking in their grandeur, and listening to the vibrance around her. *Life — it's everywhere,* she thought about the metaphor that continued to reveal itself in so many forms. Samantha slowed her pace as she made her way toward Giardino dell'Orticultura, stopping first to savor her culinary coup at the Piazza della Liberta. The luxurious park, Il Centro's northernmost point, had long been a place of respite and rejuvenation. She sat along side the pool enjoying the gentle splash from the fountain spray across her. Framed on one side by the Triumphal Arch, providing yet another metaphor. Samantha beamed. *Triumph. I do believe that's for me.*

Her gaze followed the outline of the elaborate structure, built to welcome Francis Stephen, Grand Duke of Tuscany. Samantha's fascination with the Arch stemmed more from the story of Francis I and his wife, Maria Theresa of Austria, than its architecture or physical setting. Maria's father broke with tradition, allowing his daughter to marry for love rather than an arranged union. Francis, a brilliant businessman, was a leader in name only. It was Maria's penchant for governing that oversaw their extensive domestic reform and continued rise in power across the region. Samantha deeply admired Maria, a commanding leader, a strong and wise woman, and a mother. They had sixteen children, including the future Queen of France, Marie Antoinette. It was the idea of their partnership that so intrigued her. Something she likened to her marriage to Michael. They'd built their own empire, relying on their individual strengths, creating so much more than either had ever imagined. How might that look, were they to go it alone — move along their own ways without each other. Or the unthinkable — with someone else. As good a place as she felt they were in, on this bright sunlit morning, so much remained unsaid.

She patted her eyes, a bit heavier with tears, staring at the Arch. *Can this be us? Can we triumph over the struggle? Will days turn into months, years, lessening the sting of these memories? You with her? Me with you?* Samantha had unwittingly shredded the delicate paper holding her pastry. Cradling pieces of the remains in one hand, she rubbed her fingers across her jeans with the other. Her jeans were strategically shredded and worn, each thread intricately woven into chaos. It conjured up an image she couldn't shake. The two of them had gotten them here, there was no one else to blame. But still, there would always be the space between them — as they'd begun — who they'd become. And the looming question — could their intent, their love, fill that space in a way to successfully put it all behind them?

Samantha decided, in that instant, that yes, yes it could. She needed to tuck those worries away and focus on the present and future. A future she'd decided to pursue early Saturday morning, as she stood under the shower, watching her tears and the memories of their life slip down the drain. She didn't want to start over, she wanted him — them. At least she wanted to try again. And today, though she could definitely admit that her ego was a part of that decision, she was committed to seeing it through — all of it. The vibration from her phone gently tugged her back to the present. *Allegra* . . . she answered as she made the ten-minute walk to the Giardino.

Her fears melted with the sound of Allegra's voice. She updated her on the treatments she'd agreed to, answering the myriad of questions Samantha asked. There was no point in pretending her fate had not been sealed with the diagnosis. Allegra drew on her intangible inner strength, faith Samantha had long admired and prayed she would be able to call up the same energy if she needed it. She listened intently, and then not at all — Allegra's words faded into the landscape — it was too much to take in one conversation. Allegra turned her attention to Samantha and Michael before Samantha had uttered a single word. Allegra comforted her with guidance and love. She didn't need to hear details, she was so in tune with Samantha it was clear — their marriage was suffering. Samantha was suffering. She shared her plan to return after Robert's graduation — come straight to Venice, and was taken aback by Allegra's response. No discouraging words, just that she'd be ready for her arrival. There would be so much to take care of. The thought stopped Samantha in her tracks, face to face with Allegra's impending death — sooner than she'd hoped. Her knees weekend beneath her as she struggled to find the words she so desperately wanted to share.

"Bella, my love, stand up, be strong. You are the most fabulous, resilient woman I've ever known. You're sad, I understand that sweetheart, but I need you now. Dig deep into that beautiful soul of yours, pull yourself together and help me — please. Good God sweet child, I will never be far from you — you should only be so lucky!"

Samantha let out a sigh, the breath she'd been holding in as Allegra carried on. It turned into a gentle laugh. She always found the silver lining, a way to make Samantha see a brighter side. Samantha felt stronger after their brief conversation, about so many things. How she would manage her grief, most importantly how she would support Allegra in her final days. And, how she would manage the uncertainties of her life with Michael. She peered through the beveled crystal panes of the Tepidario on her way to the top of the park, making a mental note to return for the floral exhibitions upon her arrival in April. Still Italy's largest greenhouse, Samantha had spent many hours here during her studies. Over the years, the garden had offered her an escape. The serenity and city views inspired her. It was the idea of seedlings — planted with the belief they'd grow, mature, become something bigger and more meaningful that Samantha held onto. She prayed she'd discover her purpose, answer her questions and renew her faith. She'd spent hours upon hours here, sketching, writing, thinking. She softly repeated Allegra's final words during their call:

"Love can consign us to hell or to paradise, but it always takes us somewhere."

Allegra admired Paulo Coelho's writings, quoting him often, "a soul for another time," she'd tell Samantha, believing him to be far too enlightened for this world. Today, Samantha would have to agree. *Love,* she pondered as she sat, looking over the old city framed by every angle of her view, pulling out her journal to record her thoughts. *What it is, what it does, who we are because of it — in spite of it — where will you take me now?* These were the questions dancing in her head this morning.

Oh Michael. His picture lit up her phone through the opening in her bag.

"Hey, where the heck are you? It's almost 6:00 — Dinner? Tonight? Did you forget?"

"I'm at the Giardino," she said, glancing at her watch, "I completely lost track of time, I'm so sorry! You're at the hotel? I'll be right there."

"No, no, I've been calling you though. I was getting worried, you weren't answering. I'm with Carlo, we'll pick you up. See you out front in ten."

"Okay, sorry to worry you, see ya soon. I love you."

Those three words felt different today. *I love you*, Sam had replied, not out of habit, but from her heart. They flowed sweetly across her lips — those three little words — so elusive in recent years. She disconnected the call, feeling more connected to him than ever. The thought of him warmed her, made her smile. She pictured him in the car on his way to pick her up, giddy almost, she rushed down the hill, across the bridge toward the entrance to be there when he arrived. She wanted to see him, be with him. None of her anxieties about tonight's dinner with Carlo and Stefania could tarnish the affection having its way with her right now. She was happy, excited even. Samantha decided that none of life's *"what-ifs"* would rain on her parade. Today, tonight and the foreseeable future would instead be filled with hope. She'd leave all of the aches behind her — Allegra, the empty house, Michael's betrayal. With any luck, maybe they'd stay there, or at least return when she was better equipped to deal with them. The car pulled up, she jumped in crawling over Carlo to get to Michael, embracing him as if for the very first time. She guessed it was like that — the first time — this time — for them . . .

"We let **life** get the best of us

and now we're stuck with the

remains of the worst of us."

Florence, Italy

TUESDAY, MARCH 14 – WEDNESDAY, MARCH 15, 2017

"Holy shit, Sam — you look fucking amazing! We might not make dinner," Michael grinned, in awe of the stunning beauty standing in front of him. Samantha stepped on to the patio wearing a black, off-the-shoulder Tom Ford dress that stopped just below her knees, mile-high Aquazzura sandals and the Bulgari necklace Michael had given her in Venice. She'd deliberately chosen a more provocative look for tonight. Stefania liked to boast that she single-handedly kept Chanel in business. Samantha predicted she'd show up in a suit, looking fabulous, as always. She was not going to try and fit in as she so often had. Samantha wasn't sure what Stefania knew, but she had every intention of making a statement that evening. She and Michael were there together and on her terms. She was done with that game. If they were going to make it they were going to be a team — so tonight it was all about the offense. Samantha was confident in her decision and in her strength. The road could wind wherever it liked, even take her to the cliff's edge, but she'd be ready for the journey.

Michael handed her a glass and poured a 2000 Barolo Riserva Monfortino. They laughed as it began to spill over. His eyes made their way down — inch by inch — then back up to meet her gaze, blinking from the spark of sunlight reflecting her necklace. "Cheers to us, baby." His jubilance filled the air, the deal was sealed, and Samantha was here with him. It had been a good day, better than most he could recall. They giggled as each shared their day, hers a bit less joyful given Allegra's conversation. Michael was thrilled to hear of her decision to return so quickly. He stepped behind her as she spoke, wrapping her in his arms, resting his head on her shoulder. The last four days, he had no idea what would happen when he opened Pandora's Box Saturday morning. But tonight, they seemed solidly in tact, so maybe it was all worth the risk. He relaxed as they made their way to the restaurant to meet Stefania and Carlo.

Their car pulled up to Via Ghibellina 87, once the grand Palazzo Ciofi-Jacometti, now home to the Relais Santa Croce hotel and Enoteca Pinchiorri. It was owned and operated by Michael's longtime friend Giorgio Pinchiorri. They met back when he was the sommelier at Enoteca Nazionale and the friendship grew, no doubt, from their mutual love of wine and their passionate vision of life. Samantha imagined he'd be a welcome partner in the Sesto project and wondered if Michael had already approached him. Giorgio had partnered with French Chef Annie Feolde, now his wife, to open Enoteca Pinchiorri in 1972. First as a wine bar, but it quickly evolved into the only three-star Michelin restaurant in Tuscany. Though wildly successful, it suffered near total destruction from a firebomb in 1992. Samantha considered the enormity of those events as they walked through the lobby, but so much of the original spirit of the Palazzo was still present. Giorgio's treasured wine cellar, containing over 4,000 labels, was all but destroyed in the fire. They set out to rebuild from the ashes and just a year later received their third Michelin star. *So*, Samantha thought to herself, *no matter the gravity, if you are determined you will not only survive all that life throws at you, you will flourish.* It was a concept she could relate to all too well. She also had such profound respect for Annie, a world-renowned chef, the first female chef in Italy to receive the honor, a wife and a successful businesswoman. A deep sigh followed that thought. Samantha could write the next chapters of her life as she saw fit and as she believed tonight, she absolutely would.

Of course, Stefania and Carlo were seated. Stefania always tried to arrive early to determine seating and wine selection, more of her control issues. Samantha shrugged them off. She watched her as they settled into their seats, Sam across from Michael, Carlo to her right and Stefania against the wall with a full view across the dining room. Stefania was ill at ease — edgy even, Samantha surmised, as she watched the typically cool and controlled Stefania fidgeting in her seat. She excessively looked at her phone. Samantha quickly turned to Michael to see if perhaps the interaction was with him. But no, Michael, already enjoying his wine, showed no signs of the uncomfortable angst he nearly drowned in Friday night. This did ease her fear that it was Stefania he'd been cavorting with all this time. That thought really did make her nauseous as she gave her own glass a good swirl. Good to know he hadn't gone there after all.

"Ahhh, always . . . " Samantha smiled as she read aloud, the restaurant's slogan. "A Feast for the Senses. Allegra used to tell me that Italy is a place to taste the joy of living — how right she is."

Samantha held her glass eye level peering through the crystal, across to Michael as she continued, "Some of us take that a bit too literally, yes?" offering up a smug grin as she lifted her glass in silent toast.

Tonight was not so much strained as it was off. Stefania was distant and preoccupied. With Michael and Carlo clearly celebrating their newest beginning, her behavior just didn't fit the occasion and Sam was damned obsessed with trying to figure out why. But any conversation she initiated with Stefania was met with succinct answers, even dismissal. Samantha wondered if she and Carlo had had an argument earlier. That would explain so much. Stefania only allowed one public perception of their marriage and that was absolute perfection — the happy, successful, blissfully wedded couple. Samantha never bought any of it — with anyone for that matter. Glass house couples were always the first to shatter. She would marvel at the echoes of shock and horror when it would happen . . . *"Not them, they were so happy." "Can you believe so and so? An affair? Stunned!"* The Highland Park gossip queens would spend hours hashing out the whys and whats of everyone's failed unions while doing their level best to keep their own crumbling fairytales from falling under too much scrutiny. That said, tonight was particularly strange and Samantha would get to the bottom of it. Carlo was generally upfront with Michael and Michael would tell her if she asked. After watching Stefania all night, she would ask, she would most definitely ask. Lucca, the pastry chef, brought out dessert — beautiful surprises along with Samantha's favorite strawberries and tomatoes with olive oil and balsamic vinegar.

Samantha was relieved for the evening to come to an end. It had, for the most part been uneventful, boring even, save for the fabulous meal and wine. Regardless, she could barely tolerate Stefania's strangeness throughout the night. Samantha was sure she caught Michael's eyes glaring toward Stefania which further annoyed her. But it was her behavior as they were leaving that topped it all off. Stefania waved to another couple — who'd just been seated. The woman looked familiar, though Samantha couldn't place the face. Her male companion was decades younger and drop-dead gorgeous, she'd have to admit, trying not to stare. He was the dark wavy haired, green-eyed, chiseled hunk of perfection that was the Italian male stereotype. The romance novel cover-boy. *Hmmmm,* Samantha thought, *how does that happen!?!* Stefania nearly knocked her over moving in to hug the woman as she stood to greet them.

"Darling, what a surprise, here you are in Florence. How fabulous to see you."

Okay, Samantha thought, *now you're really losing it.* Stefania so overplayed this greeting, oozing contrived surprise and love. Samantha wanted to smack her.

"My friend Alessandro insisted we dine here," the woman said.

She gushed over him as she made the introduction. *What the fuck,* Samantha thought, *is this really happening? Who acts like this?*

Michael stepped behind Samantha, tucked his arm around her waist, and guided her towards the exit. *Good, I'm not the only one who thinks this is absurd.* She lay her hand atop his as they began to walk.

"Have a lovely evening my friend, I'll call you in the morning," gushed Stefania.

The woman kissed Stefania, then leaned over to hug Michael. He brushed her off as he pulled Samantha ahead of him, but she paused briefly to watch them. Her fragrance lingered.

"Ciao, Carolina, Alessandro enjoy." Stefania blew a kiss and waved before turning around to kiss Carlo.

And then it hit Samantha, Carolina — the woman she'd seen Friday night at Rivoire. Not seen as much as intruded upon, listening to her very private conversation of marriage, divorce and new love. *Fuck, that's why she was staring at me so, she remembered me — the rude American.* Samantha took a breath as she tried to make sense of the night's weirdness. And it did make sense in that moment. She wondered if that was the married man she spoke of or someone new. She was beautiful and elegant, but quite a bit older than him. When Samantha recalled the conversation on the patio she'd imagined this woman's married lover to be much older. *"Funny thing, our imagination, it tells us exactly what we need to hear at any given moment."* Samantha heard Allegra's words of wisdom whispering to her. She'd forgotten Michael's hand around her waist and nearly tripped over him as they approached their waiting car. Samantha looked at him, his hand at her waist, but he was somewhere else. His body with her, him? Nowhere to be found.

"Hey!" She pulled on him for attention.

"Ha, sorry babe, lost in thought. Tonight was . . . "

"Fucking weird, what the hell was up with Stephanie?" Samantha interrupted.

"Damned if I know, you know how she gets."

"Gets, my ass! She was off the planet crazy. That scene as we left? Her long lost friend? Seriously? So phony, I really can't stand her, Michael. She . . . "

"I know you two don't have the greatest relationship, but you've got to let it go, we are connected, more than family and now with Sesto . . . "

"I know, Michael, I have to get along, broken record, I get it. I do it, I'm always the one trying. She's a fucking phony bitch and you know it. I get so sick of all her bullshit. Tonight was just beyond bizarre, do you think she's on meds?"

"Sam! Stop it."

Michael tuned her out, watching the streets pass as they drove. Sam's tirade was making it impossible to think. This was no coincidence, Stefania had outdone herself tonight. He'd listened to Sam over the years, her complaints about Steph's manipulations and deceit, ignoring it most of the time, writing it off the rest. But tonight, he bore the brunt of it. Stefania crossed the line —*fuck her,* he thought, *she will answer for this.* He turned back to Samantha who was intently watching him. *Something is very wrong,* she thought, *there must be more to what just happened, but what?*

Samantha was at a complete loss and could see that Michael was not in a mood to discuss any of it. Silence accompanied them the rest of the ride, the walk to the room, a heavy, troublesome silence. Michael walked away from Samantha without a word, closed the bedroom door and headed to the shower, to escape. Samantha poured herself a drink. Everything that had happened earlier raced through her head. There was simply no reasonable explanation for his sudden change in behavior after dinner. She flung herself backward, lying amongst his strewn clothes, rolling into his shirt. Then she remembered that Allegra had sent a text while they were at dinner. She lifted up her phone to read, and smiled to herself. *Another Coelho quote — oh Allegra, you angel.*

> *"Life has a way of testing a person's will, either by having nothing happen at all or by having everything happen at once."*

Samantha relaxed back into Michael's shirt, bringing it to her lips, she inhaled deeply . . . and then just as suddenly, coughed, her breath stuck to the back of her throat.

Sitting up sharply, she threw the shirt across the room — and in an uncharacteristic fit of adolescent insecurity and fury she grabbed his phone from the nightstand and began scrolling through his texts. Frantically searching, words, names and there it was — *"Carolina"* — a one-word contact that shifted the tangential axis of her world, launching it into spiraling madness. She read as she scrolled, heartbreak turned into rage. Michael casually opened the bathroom door, refreshed from his shower, and she extended her arm, offering his phone nestled in the palm of her hand. Her glares pierced him as he took it from her, knowing full well what she'd seen.

"Not quite the story you fed me Saturday morning," bitterness coldly dripping from her lips.

"Sam, it's not . . . "

"Stop it, Michael, just stop it. Everything you said, how you'd *"ended it"* blah-blah-blah. She's either one seriously delusional lunatic or you're the lying, self-centered bastard I came over here to leave. And Stephanie? Carlo? You all knew each other? How much time did you spend together? Did you love her, DO you love her?" Questions flooded Samantha. She shouted them all, one after the other, not waiting for answers. Two women inside her — at odds — one demanding to know every sordid detail, believing that only then could she put this behind her, and the other wanting to run as far away as possible. Not wanting to know anything except that it was over and that they could begin to heal. The ineffable sadness engulfed her as she sat motionless, now speechless as she tried to process this current version of the truth. How many more were there? Would he tell her, would she ask, did she care? Was this really such a shock? Seeing it, and reading it was more than she'd bargained for.

"Sam," Michael's voice was startlingly calm as he sat down next to her. "I promised to tell you anything you asked, everything you wanted to know — you've called the shots on that. I have no answer for what happened tonight — Stefania's setup. I can't possibly know her motivation to hurt you, to hurt Carolina."

"Don't say her name like that — I don't want hear it — and I don't give a fuck how hurt she might be."

"I just mean that I don't know why, but I will get to the bottom of it."

He clasped his hands behind his head, distraught, considering the aftershocks from Stefania's antics. *What was she thinking, why now?* Michael inhaled deeply. "Sammie, there is nothing left between us, I did end it. I did make it clear, you read my texts — you can see that. She is in love, I can't help that."

"Oh, you could help that — you could have stopped *"that"* before it started, you could have said no. You could have . . . "

"Don't sit there, so sanctimonious and tell me you've never — ah! Friday night, when I got to Rivoire, the guy whispering in your ear, what the fuck was that?"

"Oh my God, Michael, are you seriously gonna compare the two? My flirting at a bar and your year-long affair? You say she loves you, are you telling me you don't, you didn't love her?" Samantha got up, pacing the room as she continued, "I know, just a lapse in judgement, right? Conveniently forgetting your wife and family at home. She knew about us. I heard her say so."

"What do you mean you heard her?" He was completely at a loss now — what else did she know and how?

"Friday, when I was waiting for you. I overheard two women on the patio. One talking about her beautiful *"love"*,

Samantha exaggerated the words in air-quotes. "How she'd suffered from her ex-husband and now, even though the guy was married, they had it all. Fuck — Fuck — Fuck! Of course she had it all — all mine — everything! And you know the craziest part of all? I was struck by her elegance *and* her perfume!" As she spoke, it hit her straight on. "You son of a bitch! The Fragonard, did you buy it for me because you liked it on her? Or did she get the benefit of my good taste? Same brand different scent, how fucking thoughtful you are. That's why you were late, you were with her! Her scent was all over you."

A gust of wind blew through the villa, sending a chill up her spine. Shaking her head, she looked down at the bottle of Diamont cradled in her hand. As she lifted it up, vitriolic contempt pouring out of her, she glared back at Michael and flung it at him with every ounce of strength she had. Two things happened the instant it flew from her fingertips — first, she regretted throwing it. What if it hit him, hurt him? And then, as his college football instincts kicked in, he easily caught it overhead, and pulled it in to his chest, laughing uncontrollably. Laughing as she hadn't heard him laugh in ages — real, uninhibited, albeit nervous laughter. To which she responded with an equally boisterous outburst. How, in the depth of this darkness, could this be their reaction? Frozen, they stopped, fell silent and stared. Not the movie closeup that leaves you wanting, wondering. No, this was a mutual longing for answers. What were they doing here? What would come next?

Samantha broke the spell, dropping her head she scanned the floor, listening to the storm outside — letting it drown out the one building inside her. She left him, left the bedroom and walked straight out into the eye of it standing, numb on the patio. Lightning flashes illuminated the sky. She'd have to have be totally honest with herself. She'd never share this with Michael. The pathetic truth wreaking havoc with her right now was not the affair, it was Carolina — her age. Jesus, she was at least five — ten years older, Samantha cringed. How could he? She'd conjured up the entire imaginary scenario that sucked him in, a relentless, thirty-something bubble head with a kid or two, looking for daddy, for herself and her kids, and a bank account to secure her greedy dreams. This scenario Samantha could swallow, the overwhelming temptation. But Carolina was older, had her own life and financial security. Dreams that didn't need Michael. How did she compete with that — get over that — forget that? What would this mean to their chance for recovery? She really did believe Michael, that he was remorseful, sorry, sad, ready to water the grass they'd planted almost 30 years ago. To give his attention where it should have been all along — to her — to them. But could she completely, unconditionally reciprocate and forgive? She hated him right now, but she knew that wouldn't last either. *And there it is,* she thought, *the line in the sand, there's love, and just inches away — hate. Dance on either side of it, hover above it, writhe beneath it or try and rub it out all together. The choice comes down to which side you can live with, which one you want to lose the least.*

Michael joined her, draping a robe across her soaked back. They stood together amidst the now torrential downpour, his hands atop her shoulders which felt so slight and vulnerable to him. He was engulfed in self-hatred and admonishment. That he'd even suggested her conduct was on par with his disgusted him. He knew it was a futile attempt to lessen his guilt and it was bullshit. He was acutely aware of his absence and what doors that may have opened for Samantha, but he also believed her. She'd never betrayed him or disregarded their marriage the way he had. He'd begun to cry, his tears blinding him as the rain poured down. He was wrought with anxiety, wrestling with his breath to regain composure when her gentle touch, holding his face in her hands, guided him back to the present. He could see her and feel her. She saved him just then, in a way he'd never be able to articulate. He didn't need to, he just needed to know she was there. He lifted her on to his lap as he slid onto the wet chair, hugging her into him. He knew now just how much his life depended on their being together. He'd never let anyone or anything come between them again.

Samantha burrowed into Michael's chest, they had their work cut out for them. She hoped she could make it through, she didn't want to be one of those wives who stayed, feigning forgiveness, all the while punishing him day in and day out, staying to maintain a lifestyle they couldn't bear to let go of. *Who does that ever benefit,* she wondered. She'd always promised herself that if push came to shove, she'd jump down the rabbit hole and pray for a happy ending. An honest life alone had to be better than one spent pretending. Punishing him for the next 20 years would be an equal or far worse punishment for her. This was her deepest fear.

"Michael, we can try — I will promise you this right here, right now. That I'll try, but that's all I've got right now — I don't know where that leaves us. It will come up, things will happen, bring me back to this," flailing her arms wildly, "to *her.* I don't know, I don't know."

Samantha lowered her head, shaking it back and forth as if that would provide her the answers she so desperately sought. Knowing it wouldn't, she stopped, kissed him, took his hand, and led him inside. They made love, there on the floor, the doors to the gardens wide open, to a soundtrack of rain and wind and the crackling of thunder and lightning across the stillness of the night. The storm, their storm rolled on — over and through them, lulling them into sleep — to their dreams. Michael prayed that she would stay, would forgive him, would let it be. Samantha tried to slow the carousel down, stop the spinning — the back and forth — stay or leave — forget and forgive. To believe that they could survive this and be better for it. To believe, she could do that . . .

"Who are we,

now that life has had

its **way** with us?"

Florence, Italy

WEDNESDAY, MARCH 15 – THURSDAY, MARCH 16, 2017

The down pillow sank under the pressure of Michael's arm, as he lay, propped up, watching Sam still sound asleep. He gently pulled the duvet over her shoulders. He'd managed all of an hour or so of shut-eye, playing and re-playing dinner, running through each and every scene from the night, trying to get a clear picture of the whats and the whys. He refused to believe that Stefania, even with all her *"faults"*, would deliberately orchestrate the meeting. What would she gain in the end? He knew she'd grown fond of Carolina. They seemed to have developed a relationship separate from his. This, he believed, was the impetus for her adamant push against him and her insistence that he tell Sam about their affair. He'd ignored several of her texts and calls over the weekend, not feeling compelled to "*answer" to her* about his marriage. In retrospect, that may have been a bigger mistake than he'd considered. It was hard to fathom though, that she'd risk their history, the future that lay in front of them all, for some sort of sadistic thrill. Maybe there was more to the angst between Sam and her than he knew. But still, it just wasn't her. Stefania was inherently insecure. Other's opinions and perceptions of her were too important to take a chance for what could have been a far bigger embarrassment to all of them, in one of her favorite restaurants. But, to Sam's point, she was not herself all night. He'd seen it too, so what the hell was going on?

The most efficient way to get to the truth was, unfortunately, also the riskiest. He had to call Carolina. He didn't have the time or energy to wade through Stefania's dramatics, knowing that she'd have him jumping through hoops of fire, doling out bits and pieces, making him grovel before divulging the full story. He wanted answers and he wanted to settle things before Sam left in the morning. He certainly hadn't intended for their last day together to end on this note. He looked at the clock, 1:30 p.m., no more procrastinating, he slid out of bed, closed the doors and quietly ducked outside while scanning the grounds, then back toward the villa before punching in her name. It was still on speed dial, *fuck, I gotta change that.* He wasn't even sure Carolina would take his call, as it began to ring — once — twice . . .

"Buongiorno."

"Hi . . . " he whispered, "can you talk?"

"Sure, I thought I might hear from you today. I'm so sorry about last night. How are you?" Carolina's voice was gentle, he knew how much he'd hurt her, and yet, here she was, as kind and gracious as the first night they'd met. Guilt gripped him, dwelling upon the choices he'd made this past year. So many lives affected, none for the better. He'd have to find peace with himself if he were to move on. How could he possibly expect Sam to get past it all if he couldn't. He'd have to find a way — not to forget, but to forgive himself, but how — especially hearing Carolina's voice. He did care for her, deeply regretting where he'd left her. Sam nailed it. He could have said no, should have stopped all of it on that first night. But the "*would-haves*" were a waste of time now. He did it and he had to live with the mess of it all.

"What did Stefania do? Why were you there? How . . . "

"Let me stop you right there, Michael. Last night was not about Stefania — or you — for that matter. Alessandro is my daughter's friend, visiting from Milan." Her voice changed, a self-assured air replaced the calm he'd first heard. She found satisfaction feeling Michael's sense of relief upon learning that Alessandro wasn't her lover.

"He asked to go there, having heard so much about Giorgio's wine cellar. Surely you know how close Stefania and I have become?"

"I do now!"

Michael jumped on her sentence, annoyed and impatient.

"So you both planned your *"meet and greet"* as we were leaving to humiliate my wife? Me?"

"Oh, Michael, your arrogance is so unbecoming. Your ego really is something beyond my comprehension."

Her cool exterior finally cracked, the pain he'd inflicted flowing out of her. "I am done here. Stefania is a remarkable, loyal woman — to her husband, to you. I know it was she who urged you to tell your wife. But not for protection of either of you. She is a dear friend. My friend!

She couldn't stand seeing me stuck in your web any longer. Her anxiousness last night? It was her grave concern for all of us. I'd told her we would be dining there. She had no way of changing your plans without stirring up questions if there would be a crossover. I did shift our reservation to a later time. I wanted to enjoy my meal and, frankly, not have to look at you and your wife — your *"happy little life"* through the night."

"I'm so sorry, I . . . " Michael interjected.

"Please, don't. You are sorry, but not for your actions, you don't possess an ounce of empathy or care for anyone but yourself. I suspect you will find a practical resolution with your wife, only because you've decided that is what you want now and your life will go on as though I never existed. Not so easy for most of us. I will always carry you in my heart, Michael. Hopefully, a reminder of what not to do, who not to be. You have been a deliciously horrid lesson, one I will never forget. Goodbye, Michael . . . "

The faint click from her phone would close this chapter in his life, for now, but it was her final words, ringing in his head that he couldn't stand. He wasn't all those things, that person she described, the man she despised so venomously. She'd see that one day. He had cared about her, but he just couldn't leave, not for her. There was too much between him and Sam, too much to throw away. A history, a family, a life, a relationship he would vow to save, if she'd let him.

"Who was that?" Samantha asked, standing behind him. She knew full well who it was but needed to hear it from him. He looked at her, consumed with worry. How long had she been standing there, had she been listening inside, how much did she overhear? She'd heard more than she'd bargained for, more than she'd ever let him know. What a curious parallel, trying to absorb their conversation. Her husband talking to his lover — the tenor in his voice, the words between them — the stark reality of it all. Theirs was a casual comfort, the kind that grows from spending time together. Nuanced gestures as he spoke, the tone in his voice. They'd been a couple, until last week, if she took him at his word regarding their breakup. Samantha stiffened, listening to Michael talk, watching him. She didn't doubt his love for her, his desire to put the year behind him, to come back to their marriage. But how does this just disappear? How does he forget the woman he'd spent his time with, shared his secrets with, his body and soul, all these months? Where would he put those feelings? How would he manage that and dedicate his energy to her, to their marriage?

And what about their marriage — their 25 years together? Where did that fit into all of this? It wouldn't be any easier to disregard that investment of time and emotion, regardless of how fragmented the present had become. She knew that in the end, she wouldn't just walk away, close door number one and pick another. She also knew in her heart that Michael wouldn't turn his back that seamlessly either. Well, Michael, she thought smugly, *you drug us into this pile of shit, at least you will have to wade through it all as well.* As confident as Samantha felt in his want of it all, she wasn't nearly as convinced in his ability to do it. Anyone's for that matter. You stray, you open yourself up, in search of something — love, sex, yourself — not because you've got it all, but precisely the opposite. You don't think you have any of it and you desperately want it. She'd struggled with those yearnings for months herself, still not completely sure this was the answer. So how on earth did she expect Michael and Carolina to shut it all down. She feared Carolina's emotional attachment more, because she didn't know the full extent of their relationship. She had only the surface answers Michael had provided, and as hard as she was trying to let that be enough, it might not be. At some point, she may have to ask and be ready to hear the full scope of their relationship.

She reflected on Allegra's imagination theory, *"We do see only what we choose, create the reality we can live with."* Overhearing his conversation just now drove home the notion. She could change the depth of emotions, the level of involvement, the story, so she could survive. She found a new appreciation for those suffering from PTSD. The mind, that miraculous grey matter, really does its best to protect the heart through the most unimaginable experiences. This would take more effort to process, more to get past, to work through. *Goddamn you, Michael, why didn't you just say no!*

"Sit down please, we need to talk," Michael said softly. He pulled out a chair and told her exactly what he'd done, what Carolina had said. Samantha listened patiently, extending an unbearable silence before responding, relieved that he'd told her the truth, at least what she'd heard from his side of the conversation. This was actually a speed bump moment. Had he lied, she would have known exactly what to do next. But he was truthful, as he'd promised he'd be going forward. For them to have any shot at all, this was significant.

"Hmmmm," she sighed, "I'm trying really hard to keep all of my emotions separate, so *please* don't interrupt me."

There was so much he'd just dumped on her. So many unanswered questions, pent up anger, sadness coming at her from every direction. She'd start with the evening itself and Stefania.

Michael nodded.

"I was up most of the night, starting at the beginning, obsessing — ad nauseam, no surprise there." She chided her own perceived shortcomings. "The whole damn night, none of it made sense. Stefania, you, *her* — "

"Babe . . . "

"Michael! Shut up! Listen to me . . . Let. Me. Talk."

He stopped, her admonishment was well deserved, but it was so hard for him at times. His thoughts raced ahead at lightening speed while she deliberated every thought and word before she spoke. It could take her forever to get her point across and he wanted to know the end of the story, right now.

"I actually wondered about that. Stephanie, I don't believe she would be so purposefully mean, regardless of the fact that we are not and have never been particularly close. She has been a part of your life for so long, it just didn't add up. That and the fact that I don't think she's inherently evil, just stupid and superficial." Samantha paused to change gears while shifting nervously in her seat, these were not conversations she liked. The hard stuff. Her comfort zone lay somewhere in-between — knowing the problems at hand, but preferring to let them sort themselves out rather than moving through them. But here she was, ready to lay it all out, face the challenges, fight, get it all out on the table and work through it. "So Carolina and her daughter's friend, cute. Were you jealous?"

"Sam!"

"Michael!" She mimicked him and continued, "I actually do believe that. I just didn't ever want to be face to face with the woman you've been cheek to cheek with."

Michael smiled to himself, she did have a way with words. He loved her dry, quick wit.

"At any rate, now I have a face, a voice to put with your stories and it fucking sucks. You fucking suck!"

She inhaled slowly, deeply working to keep her composure, and not cry as she continued. "Tell me, Michael, how did we become guests in each other's lives? I felt like the intruder last night. I see now that there was more to you all than you're telling me. This wasn't a casual, once in awhile thing. But I don't want more details. I just have to find a place for all of it, so I can get on with my life. I don't want to find myself swimming in the unanswered questions. Second guessing every move you make, every call you take. Jesus, I'm channeling Sting now." She huffed, "But seriously, I mean it, texts, calls, I'll drive myself crazy, I can't do that, I won't do that — to either of us." *Oh, Michael, it would have been so much better if you had just fucked her that night and never looked back.* She lowered her head, she was done, spent, ready to put it all away — once and for all — mostly because that was the only choice she saw for herself. She'd made the decision to stay, to give their marriage one last shot. The talking points didn't change, they were simply circling back, saying the same things, using different words. No complete resolution would be found in one more conversation. It would ultimately come down to action — how they went forward from here. Step by step, putting all the tears and talks to work. Would it work? Only time would tell. Therein lay her biggest fears. Had she set the stage for this during Steven's senior year? She had seen, and ignored the changes.

But not one aha! moment — not a single incident that would suggest disrupting your life of twenty-some odd years was an obvious or necessary choice. No, it creeps up on you, one day at a time, while you're busy living. You're getting the kids off to school, making sure you've chosen all the right schools, deciding what sports they play, what food they eat, how they spend their time, who they spend their time with. Toddler charms blur into adolescence. All this becomes the way you spend your days, make your friends. You unwittingly drift into the drive-by conversations with your spouse about things that mean everything to you on any given day and very little to him. He's interested in the "big stuff", but to you it's all "big stuff" and you resent the implication that his days are more important than yours. He's busy navigating through his own life challenges — financial decisions, business growth, meetings, travel, people. Some you do know, others remain a flurry of names and titles whose paths you'll never cross. Life choices you're told you have a part in making, but the seat at the table is always occupied. And

honestly, you're not even sure of what you bring to the table anymore, so you're perfectly willing to accept that place, as long as your bubble remains intact. Content with your place in the "need to know" line.

Until one day you wake up, alone, in an empty house and wonder how that happened — asking yourself how you were not better prepared. You, the girl with the plan — the survivor — the one who always found the silver lining and made the best of it. Gone are the meticulously organized days and full house, every hour and activity accounted for and planned well in advance. Along with the urge or even the need to get out of bed in the morning. You don't "have" to be anywhere, for anyone at any given time. But you convince yourself that you're busy with your life, your friends, your everyday. It's somewhere in there that everything gets mixed up, lost — the black hole sucks in your "to have and to hold", and spits out let's just "get on with it"—"it" being the business of surviving. Surviving everything life throws at you. Not that there aren't good times, fond memories, but at some point the memories gain prominence and you find yourself dwelling in the past as a means to justify the present. Others had warned you about it, you'd read about it, seen countless movies about it — but that was them, not you! You'd never be one of "those" women, "those" mothers who couldn't fathom a life once their children had gone off to college. The ones who chased youth, freedom, another life. Not you! You were happily married, educated, pretty, social, fun — you'd be fine. Dumb-ass! You weren't fine, and you're not fine. How foolish of you to ignore the flagrant warnings. Everything that was just plain annoying before your last child moved into his dorm, had now taken on catastrophic dimensions. Those "drive-by" conversations were the only words you shared and you had absolutely no patience for any of them.

If it's true that your kids are the third party in your marriage, then their departure leaves a cavernous hole from which you hope to emerge. You assume that you'll stroll out together, hand in hand, and pick up where you left off before parenting became your only common ground. It never occurred to you that you might not make it out of the vapid chasm you'd fallen into. That even the smallest gestures of attention, affection toward each other would become so awkward, require so more effort than either of you were willing to extend. So days turned into weeks, weeks into months of contrived love and pretense. Suddenly happily ever after seemed more of an unattainable childhood dream than anything even close to resembling your current union. The two of you are more like strangers than significant others — conversations as empty as the now vacant rooms in your home. That separateness replaced the kids — it became your new, unwelcome "partner", aggressively moving in and taking over.

And then late one morning, sipping your espresso, immersed in self-pity and indifference, you hear your voice, at first a whisper, begging you to listen. 'Where have you gone?' Over 25 years of learned behavior, essentially snuffed out. The reason you two don't talk is because at some point you just stopped caring. And you replay the years of your acquiescing — his talking over you, interrupting you. You allowed it to silence you. Your means of coping was to just agree, tune out. Why didn't you see it happening, why didn't you stop it? You acknowledge that you may never answer those questions fully. How is it that you went from an independent thinker to someone who just regurgitated out his opinions, ideas and dreams, embracing them all as your own. Easy, you admit finally, there was his agenda and his will and at some point all of it became too much to compete with. The boisterous "get it done" determined spirit and strength that you were so attracted to in the beginning is exactly what shut you down over the years. What you once revered, you came to loathe. And there it was . . . the fine line between love and hate — again! But that morning, you did have the time to reflect and what you understood more clearly than ever was that you desperately wanted your voice back, your seat at the table — and if not with him, if not here, then so be it.

Steven's senior year was the worst, the year you should have done something. But doing nothing "is" doing something, unintentional or otherwise. Maybe if you'd been more communicative with Michael, pressed him to acknowledge what you were feeling, encouraged him to be more a part of your home life. Maybe if you'd shown more interest in the company, his interests. Maybe if you'd taken the initiative to show him that you wouldn't sit back and just let life happen. Maybe if he'd been more present, he would have seen you slipping away, losing your way. Maybe . . .

She needed to find closure to this chapter, knowing that's what was best for her. When confronted with painful, difficult situations, she'd always processed them, tried to learn from them. She'd never settled for the wallowing victim role — the *"why me". It's me, shit happens, life happens — dwell on it and be miserable or get on with it and make*

a life worth living. She'd made that choice here and she was ready to get on with it. Last night be damned, Carolina be damned, Michael's year of living badly be damned. She was actually content with herself and her decision as she peered up through her tousled bangs, watching Michael. He spoke slowly and softly as he clasped his hands around hers, "Let It Be."

Nice choice, she thought as he said that.

"How Still My Love."

Smiling, she softly kissed him. This silly song game had become such an endearing part of their framework.

"I love you, Sammie, make me a promise?"

"Hah! Anything once, it all works once, right?!"

"We both give this everything we have, each other. And, keep talking, communication, regardless of the outcome, if we stay to keeping those lines open we can do this."

"That is a promise I will make. To talk to you, to talk!" She laughed, "I'm so tired of keeping it all inside, but you have to promise to listen, really fucking listen. This is us now, the two of us, together, not me following you, us — a team again. Can you promise me that?"

"I can, I do," Michael answered.

"Jesus, are we renewing our vows?"

Sam chuckled at the thought, but really that is what she felt happening. There, on the patio six days through hell, she began to see a light, the possibility for a fresh start. Ironically, it was for very different reasons. It occurred to her that Michael had no idea just how close she'd been to leaving him when she landed last Friday. That his perspective was based on her forgiving his affair. He sank to grief for his actions when in reality it may have been his affair that saved their marriage. She hadn't considered those ramifications until this very minute. She'd come to Florence to leave — their marriage, their past, their future really. Surely the weight of those emotions didn't just disappear. Maybe what mattered was that when she was face to face with the reality of an ending, one she wasn't responsible for, she didn't want it. What she wanted was her family, back, intact, together. Maybe that was her *"aha"* moment.

She did believe they had a chance to mend what had broken these past years. *Maybe*, she thought, tightening her fingers around his, *a good life is just learning to master the art of putting the broken pieces back together, over and over. Nothing is perfect, at least not forever. But if it was good, really good once, then with a little work it could be again.* They locked eyes, she started to speak when her phone rang.

"It's Allegra. I need to take this." Slipping her fingers loose, she walked inside.

"Hello, my beautiful girl, I've been thinking of you all morning. How are you, love?"

"Ahhhh, well, there have been better mornings!" Samantha smiled as she answered.

"Oh, darling, there will always be better mornings. But this is the one you have today. Take it for the wildest ride you can!"

"Allegra, do you believe it is possible to love two people at the same time?"

"Oh my God, yes, we should all be so lucky!" She cackled, "Samantha, absolutely my child. Why do you ask, are you feeling his heart is split?"

"Yes, no — I just wonder — you know?"

"All too well, Samantha, all too well. I do believe that different souls set your heart on fire over the course of a lifetime — for very, very different reasons. Some begin so very brightly then quickly burn out, others smolder, deeply within us — forever. Those are the ones — a blessing and a curse, because they never truly let us go."

"Hmmmm . . . maybe so."

"Samantha, what is your deepest fear? That he is loving you both, but choosing the *"devil he knows"* over what is undeniably a very big risk. That he's staying in the safe harbor, familiarity, history — they are a powerful draw you know, regardless of the temptations that present themselves along the way. And so what if he is! *HE IS!"* She deliberately enunciated her last words slowly, loudly. "He *IS* choosing your life, you. Who cares what was. We are human, you are human, my dear. Let it go. Let your worry go too. This is what you're really asking, isn't it?"

Samantha marveled at Allegra's innate ability to see through her, get to the heart of what she was thinking so quickly.

"I suppose. What do you do in the wake of it all? What do you do with all the pieces, the heartbeats you leave behind — the ones you still feel."

"Oh, my darling, you dance to them. Those who touch your soul so deeply, not everyone gets to feel that, accept it, be grateful for it — those who know such a love even once in a lifetime — sometimes an ache, sometimes a smile — they are the lucky ones. And my God, to feel it more than once! AHHHHH — no words. We are the lucky ones! I won't see you before you leave, safe travels, I am anxious for your return. I love you, Samantha, you will survive. You will be better in the end of this I am absolutely positive!"

"I love you too, please keep me posted with everything until I get back here. I will come sooner if you need me. Graduation isn't until the third week of May. I've just got a few details to confirm next week. But I don't have to stay."

"Sweetheart, I will be as fine as the day is long, don't worry so. But here's something I would like you to think about — the significance of your visit now. What you've discovered, about your relationship, but more so about yourself — all in seven days. Seven is my number — you've known that. Do you know why?"

"No, we've never really talked about it."

"It is awakening! In religion, science, spirituality, it brings everything full circle. Think about it — seven days in the week, seven principles of truth. Seven sacraments, seven chakras — I could go on and on! I just want you to consider the perspective of these seven days, what they've meant to you, what they've given you. You'll see what I mean, you will see everything so much more clearly as you reflect on this time here — now. I love you darling. Talk soon."

"Ciao."

Samantha disconnected, checking the time as she did. 4:00 p.m. *God,* she couldn't believe how quickly the day had gotten away. Just hours left here, with Michael, Florence. She now regretted the early morning flight she'd booked, wanting more time with Michael and Allegra, but she did have to get back. She could feel the ripples of relief making their way through her. Feelings she hadn't anticipated at all as she took off in Dallas a week ago. The scenarios playing out then bore no resemblance whatsoever to what she saw today. There'd be no separation, the conversations she'd rehearsed were unnecessary. That was next, she needed to learn how to stop "*the voices*", curb the unrelenting worry over situations that never materialized. She cringed thinking of the inordinate amount of time and energy that practice had occupied over the years. *What a waste. Lessons learned, I hope!* She talked herself through the next steps of her journey — home — LA — graduation planning — back to Italy. It looked doable. She would even admit that she was excited about the coming weeks. Life's stranglehold seemed to be loosening — just a bit. She wasn't so naive to think that all her emotions, concerns, and fears would suddenly disappear, but there was an overwhelming sense of hope enveloping her. She could see the proverbial light at the end of the tunnel and she was anxious to get to it. To get on with it.

"Michael." Samantha followed the sound of his razor into the bathroom.

"I love you. I do!"

"Well damn — I'm glad to hear you say that! I love you."

She dropped her robe, dropped to her knees, pulled down his boxers and took in the one, most pleasurable constant she had. Thinking of Allegra's words — one awakening these past seven days had been their physical attraction, their sexual gratification. At first, so frenetic, fearful of losing everything, sex was their lifeline. The desperate attempts of two lost souls fighting their way back.

If they could just hold on, keep each other close, the world would not have its way with them, they could survive. It was the act of letting go, stripping each other down, peeling back all the layers that did bring them closer. Ease replaced panic, fear turned to hope as love made its way through the door. She felt comfortable now, the urgency had passed, she didn't feel the need to *"save"* anyone or anything. She glanced up, satisfied as she watched Michael's body swaying in sync with her motions. Her lips grasping tighter, urging him on, she loved pleasuring him this way — much more so now. Control, she supposed, it was her time for a bit more of that. Her hands kept his at bay, not letting him change their position, she wanted this — her way. Closing her eyes, she pictured their tryst on the balcony in Venice. The reckless abandon they'd both shared under the full moon, to the sound of the canal's grand thrashing — that was it — her turning point. The vivid memory of that glorious night sent shivers through her. She stood up, wrapping her arms around his neck, allowing him to lift her onto him as he turned, setting her atop the vanity, rocking and kissing in unison — releasing into each other. It was, she thought as she buried her head into his chest, the perfect way to bring this day to an end. *Release, all of it. Let. It. Go. Let. It. Be.*

Morning's early breeze carried the scent from the kitchen staff preparing today's pastries. Samantha took a final sip of espresso and a once over the villa while Michael finished up a conference call. The car was waiting, this was goodbye for now. The drive to the airport seemed shorter than usual. She wasn't ready to leave him, definitely not ready to leave Florence. There weren't a lot of words — tightly holding each other's hands, as if the exchange of energy might lessen the fears they were both grappling with. Samantha wondered if he'd see Carolina once she left. Michael wondered if she'd re-think her resolve to stay with him. Both of them were acutely aware of the fragile ground they now occupied.

"I feel like I'm forgetting something," she spoke, thinking of Allegra's charming way to change a subject — *"So how about Africa?"* She'd interject the most unrelated thought just to change the topic when discomfort moved in. It usually worked, Samantha smiled quietly, picturing her friend.

"You always forget something!" Michael joked, "You're coming back so soon, if you did and it can't wait I'll send it off. Don't worry about it." He kissed her forehead as Fausto took her bags.

"Yeah, yeah, you know how I am about packing, this morning was so rushed. I'm fine." Samantha fought back her tears as they embraced, kissing each other, endings and beginnings. It suddenly felt so foreign, so much was at stake here. God, what a roller-coaster these past few days had been. She'd have more hours than she wanted to consider it all. Dreading the long flight home more than ever, she was glad to have their plane for the short ride to Rome.

Finally, it was Michael who broke loose, taking hold of her shoulders. "Promise me you'll talk to me. I wish I could get on that plane with you. The timing stinks. But I'm here, waiting for you — only you — to come back. Please promise me you're coming back."

"I promise, babe. I love you."

She quickly turned away, no goodbye, no looking back, no crying — not yet — she promised herself. Just get up the steps through the door, and go. But she did sneak a glimpse out the portal, once she was settled in. Michael was still on the tarmac. He hadn't moved, as if he were waiting for her to come back out. This was a memory she could hold onto and feel good about.

Michael stood, watching her. Should he go get her, go with her? Torn, but realistic, he needed to let her go, believing she'd be back and looking forward to their future together. Samantha pressed her hand to the window, smiling as they taxied on. Michael blew her a kiss as he turned, believing that the worst had passed and the *"from now on"* would work, they'd make it work — together.

She made her connection in Rome with time to spare, sending Michael a quick text before boarding:

> *"All good here, waiting to take off now. Will call when I land in Dallas. Love you."*

Then Samantha settled into her lounger, taking the flight attendant up on her offer of champagne. She was ready to drink up and tune out. A little indulgence to silence the voice in her head. There'd be time enough to sort through this latest version of reality once she was in the air. Two glasses in and they were next in line for take off. *Cheers to it all,* she toasted as the pilot made the announcement. Tucking her earbuds in, she began to scroll through her playlists, feeling a slight jolt as the wheels retracted, nose up, they soared into the clear blue sky. Samantha watched the city disappear below, before turning back to her phone, and Michael's incoming text —

> *"You were right, you forgot your notebook on the patio. I'll send it. Safe travels."*

Fuck! Samantha froze, she'd left her journal. *Oh my fucking God. Michael, what have I done?!* Anxiety consumed her. She pictured him sitting in the villa, reading, page after page — and there was not a damned thing she could do about it.

SAMANTHA AND MICHAEL'S

Music weaves its way through Samantha and Michael's story, connecting them to their past and to each other. The songs and albums listed here are an integral part of their journey.

Enjoy!

ARCANGELO CORELLI / COMPLETE EDITION

https://amzn.to/2JGhzQK

THE VERY BEST OF FLEETWOOD MAC

https://amzn.to/2JInjd3

THE VERY BEST OF THE EAGLES

https://amzn.to/2ras4nX

THE BEATLES 1967 – 1970 (THE BLUE ALBUM)

https://amzn.to/2raQxdP

TIME SPACE – THE BEST OF STEVIE NICKS
https://amzn.to/2HHdZFs

HARDEN MY HEART: THE BEST OF QUARTERFLASH
https://amzn.to/2HIqReE

BEST OF BILLY JOEL
https://amzn.to/2JIoGIJ

BEST OF BONNIE RAITT ON CAPITOL 1989-2003
https://amzn.to/2HI3mT0

THE ESSENTIAL BOZ SCAGGS
https://amzn.to/2JDZoez

THE MOTELS ESSENTIAL COLLECTION
https://amzn.to/2Ks25Bd

ULTIMATE COLLECTION: QUINCY JONES
https://amzn.to/2JD0xDk

JASON MRAZ / WE SING. WE DANCE. WE STEAL THINGS.
https://amzn.to/2r9Cswg

'80S POP HITS
https://amzn.to/2w8OkVd

'70S GOLD
https://amzn.to/2r9DBE4

Notes From The Nest

EMPTY NEST RESOURCES AND READS

My decision to write this story was based, in part, on my own empty nest experience, but also from the many friends and associates who I watched struggle when their children left the nest. As I shared my work, people opened up to me. Through these exchanges I became acutely aware of the deep emotional impact this phase of life delivers. There is no running — just learning to come to terms with 'what's next' and embracing the changes.

Notes From The Nest evolved from these conversations. It is an online community and blog, exploring pretty much every aspect of life in an "empty nest." It's a safe place to vent, question and learn. This new chapter in our lives is not an ending, but instead the beginning of a grand, new adventure. Married or single, this can be the most exhilarating time in our lives. Join the conversation — the community is gracious, diverse and growing daily!

This list is a beginning . . . I hope you will find the books and links listed here helpful as you move along your way. Stop running, and read! You are not alone!

www.melmediallc.com/notesfromthenest

melmediallc @melgreenberg17

@melgberg NotesFromTheNest

Read

The Best of Beverly Beckham: I was the sun, the kids were my planets and other reflections from the Globe columnist

http://bit.ly/2HEVFky

Empty Nest: What's Next?: Parenting Adult Children Without Losing Your Mind

https://amzn.to/2JClBKg

From Mom to Me Again: How I Survived My First Empty-Nest Year and Reinvented the Rest of My Life

https://amzn.to/2jUi2nC

The Second Half of Marriage

https://amzn.to/2I631Nl

Chicken Soup for the Soul: Empty Nesters: 101 Stories About Surviving and Thriving When the Kids Leave Home

https://amzn.to/2J3Jz5b

Explore & Connect

The Gottman Institute

www.gottman.com/blog/rescue-marriage-empty-nest-syndrome

Terry Real

www.terryreal.com

"Depression in Women: 5 Things You Should Know"

http://bit.ly/2HW2YQY

"Men and Depression"

http://bit.ly/2Ijgem8

"Coping With Traumatic Events"

http://bit.ly/2wiqFl9

MeetUp.com

www.meetup.com

Dailystrength.org

www.dailystrength.org

Emptynestsupport.com

www.emptynestsupport.com

Today.com

https://on.today.com/2w6YCVK

How to Thrive in an Empty Nest

https://nyti.ms/2rcoZVe

Ten Ways for Parents to Survive an Empty Nest

http://bit.ly/2jl6j1q

4 Things They Never Tell You About Empty Nest Syndrome

http://bit.ly/2FwVyBz

Empty Nest Syndrome: Tips for Coping – Mayo Clinic

https://mayocl.in/2w8zsWu

The End of Empty Nest Syndrome – Oprah.com

http://bit.ly/2KqTTRX

Support

HealthyWomen.org

www.healthywomen.org

Depression in Women

www.mentalhealthamerica.net/conditions/depression-women

International Foundation for Research and Education on Depression

www.ifred.org

Depression and Bipolar Support Alliance (DBSA)

www.dbsalliance.org

National Institute of Mental Health

www.nimh.nih.gov

American Psychiatric Association

www.psychiatry.org

Anxiety and Depression Association of America

www.adaa.org

Acknowledgements

Running With Our Eyes Closed saw its first light in 2016. In the months and years that followed, inspired by the heart-warming and heartbreaking stories of friends and family, Samantha and Michael came to life. They became my friends and confidants, while I created their relationship and life in the phase of their lives as empty nesters, it helped me see my own life in an extraordinary new light. There were many people who helped turn my dream into reality, and I am grateful to each and every one of them.

To my husband Dean and my sons, Matthew and Dylan — my pillars and my light — through it all. Their support was unwavering, and their love was unconditional. I am blessed beyond measure to share this life with three of the strongest, kindest, funniest, most patient men on the planet. And to my then 7-week-old German Shepherd, Grazia. When I sat down to do this — to really do this, in January 2017, she sat on my lap as I wrote — every word, every day. Her presence was a constant reminder that even in the perceived 'emptiness', life keeps moving and brings us exactly what we need and where we need to be.

To my friends, for the countless hours of laughter and tears we spent sharing our own stories of life in our empty nests. With their love and support in challenging me to turn my idea into reality, I found my voice and the determination to bring this vision to life.

To Monica Dussa, who knew that our chance meeting at the Beverly Wilshire would lead to this! She read every word from the start, and offered her insight and critical encouragement. She pushed me to reach deeper into every connection between Sam and Michael, peel away the layers, which brought such beautiful perspective to their story. To my dear friend, Dr. Sana Barada, for providing the location details and Florentine influence, and for the months we spent talking about our fragile, imperfect human condition. To my editor, and longtime friend, Kate McCormick — not enough space here! I asked her to be a part of this journey because I knew there would be total honesty. She was disciplined and tenacious in her support and provided gentle, insightful criticism of my project. Kate guided me to keep, change and let go of; too much, too little and too many commas. "For now!" — our daily mantra for it all. To Amelia Noyes, my incredibly talented cover illustrator — I knew from the first bottle of Prosecco we shared at La Piazza that she was not only the perfect woman for the job, but that our journey as friends was just beginning. And to Connie Newton, the sweet, intuitive angel who is always there to listen, advise and reaffirm the beauty of this wild ride we are all on.

Lastly, to the women and men who shared their experiences with me. They exposed their fears and hopes and dreams of where the next chapters in their lives may take them. Sam and Michael's story is fiction, but for all of us who have raised our children and now stand in an empty doorway as we send them along on their way, the void is real. It is perhaps the darkest moment in an otherwise beautifully luminous life. Overwhelmed with questions and insecurities, we ask, "What's next? Who am I? Who are we?" I discovered over the course of writing this book that the flaws and fears we all live with somehow find their way to the surface, cause us to take notice, and *that* is when the magic can happen. It is this opportunity for which I am most grateful.

About the Author

MEL GREENBERG is the married mother of two sons in their early twenties. She worked as a copywriter and producer in radio and television before having children and making the decision to stay at home with them full-time.

Four years ago she became an empty nester, and she struggled to find her voice and direction. Ultimately, it was her passion for writing and the discovery that she was not alone that led her to write *Running With Our Eyes Closed*. It is the first installment of a series exploring her characters' struggle to redefine their lives as empty nesters.

When she's not visiting her boys, and traveling the world, Mel enjoys life in the Southwest with her husband Dean, her beloved English Bulldog Bruno, and German Shepherd Grazia.

Notes

Notes

Notes